PROTEIN
MILK
BYE

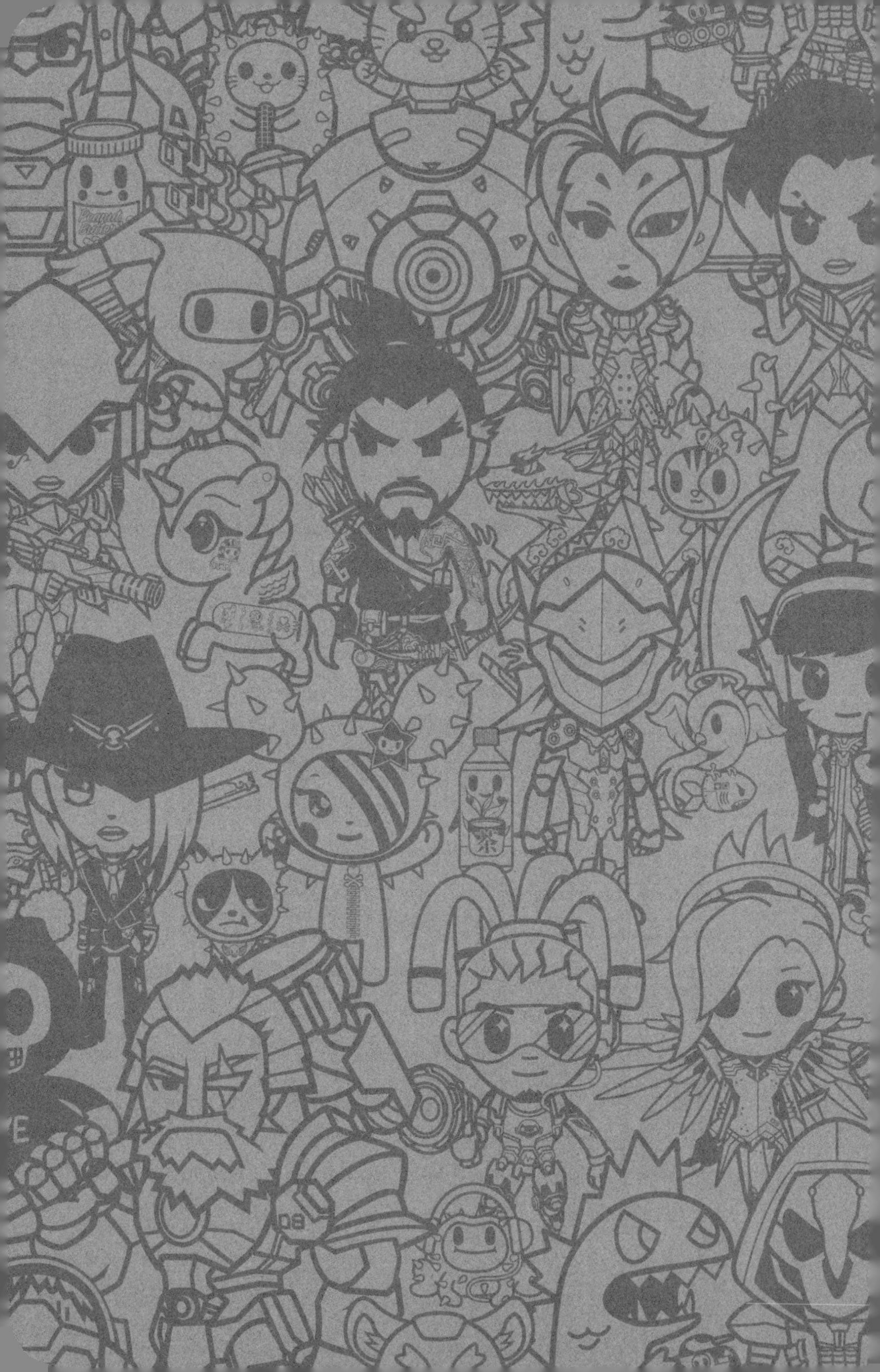

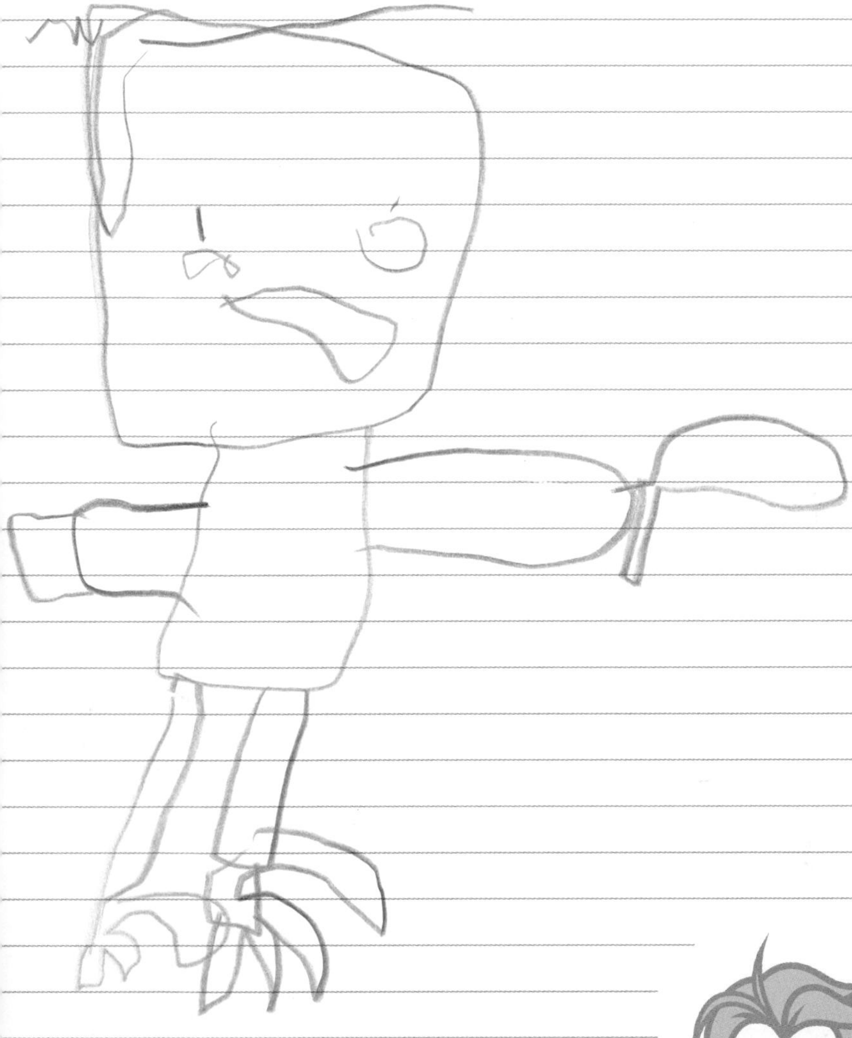

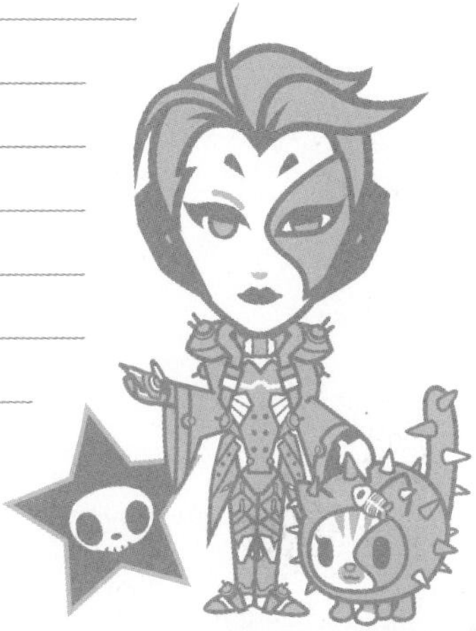

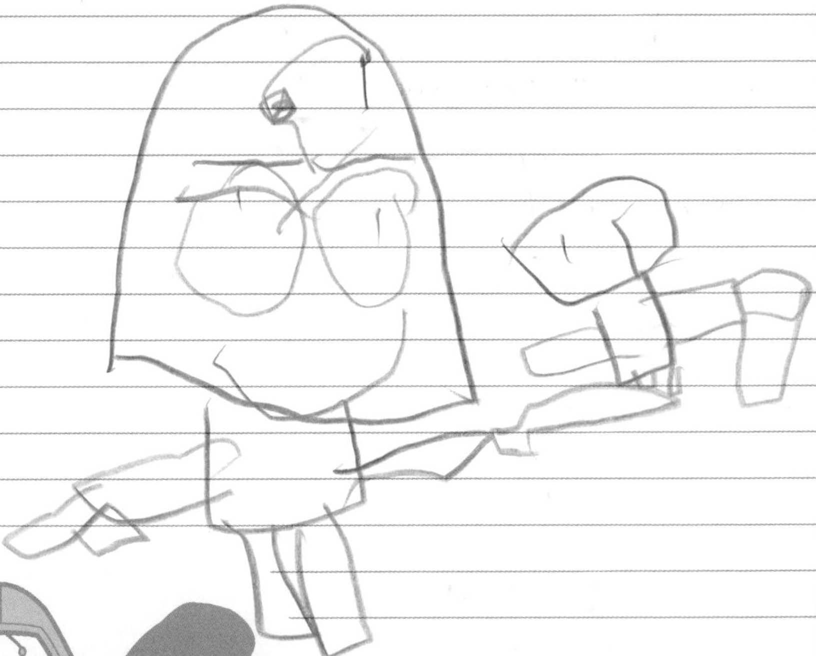

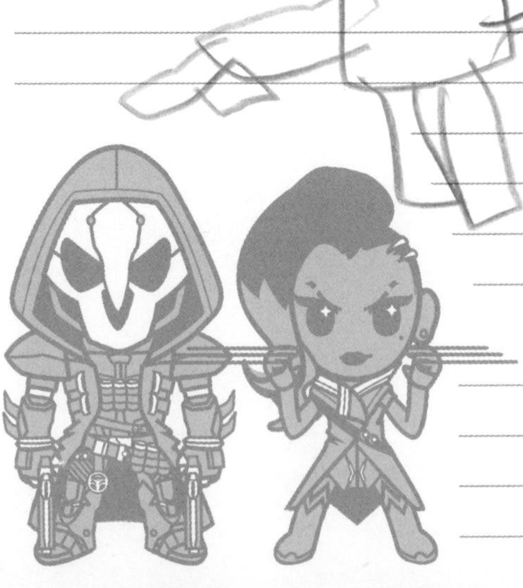

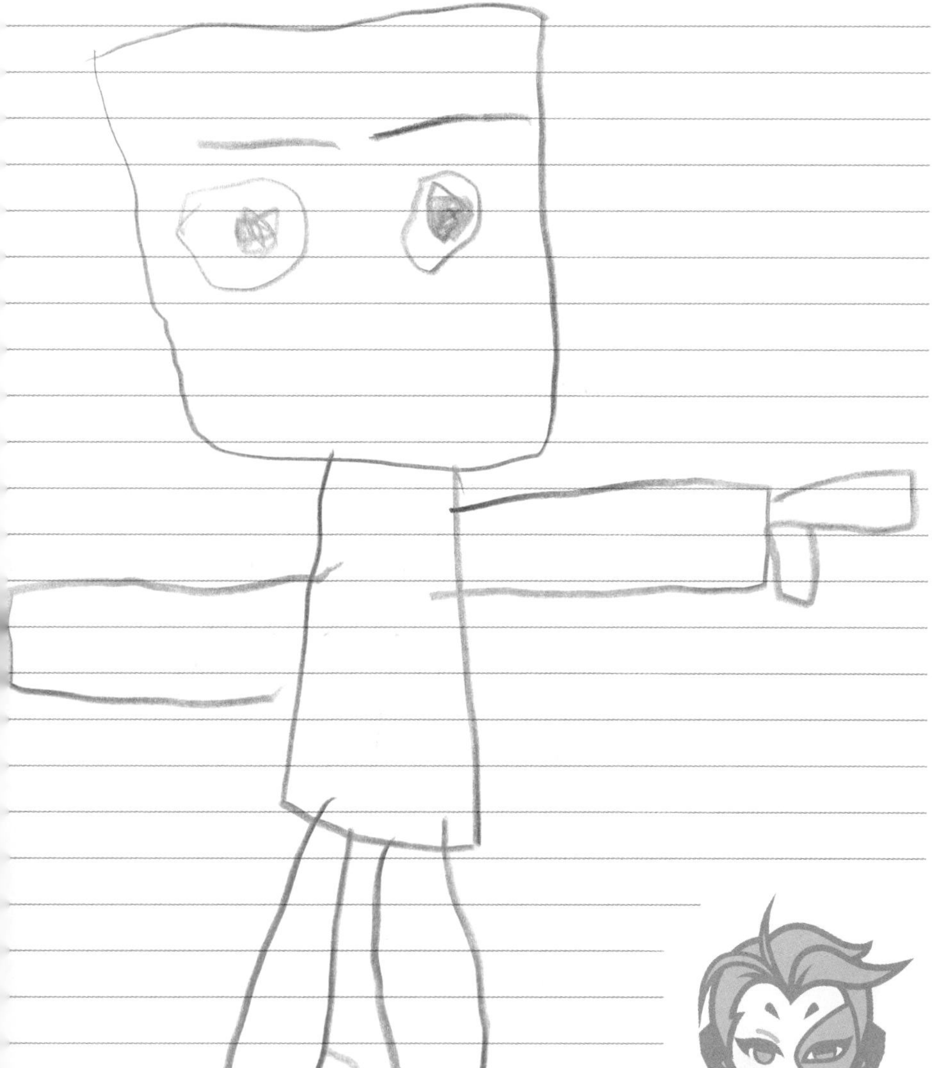

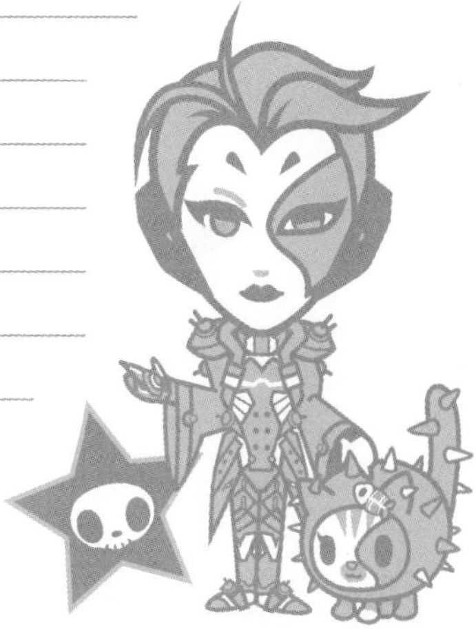

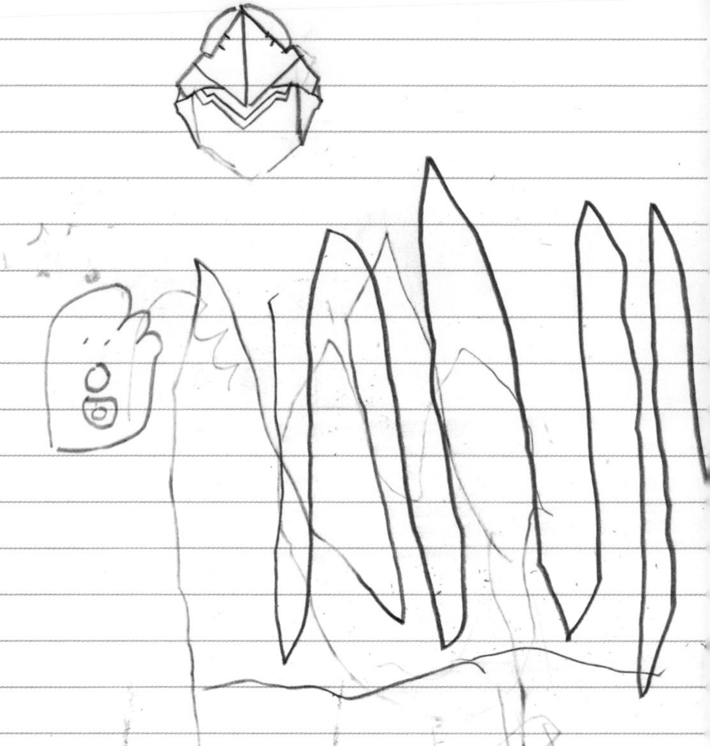

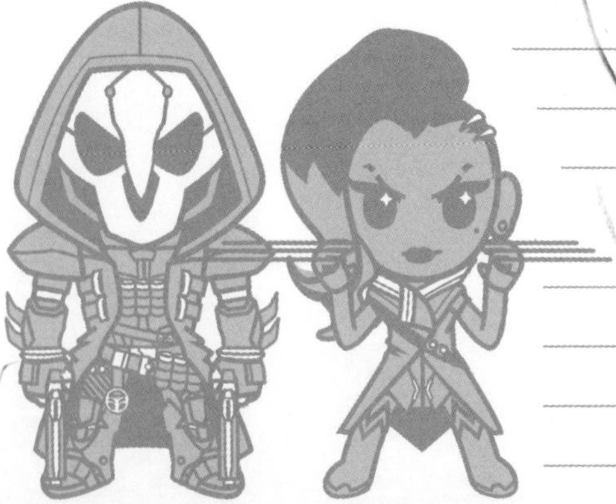

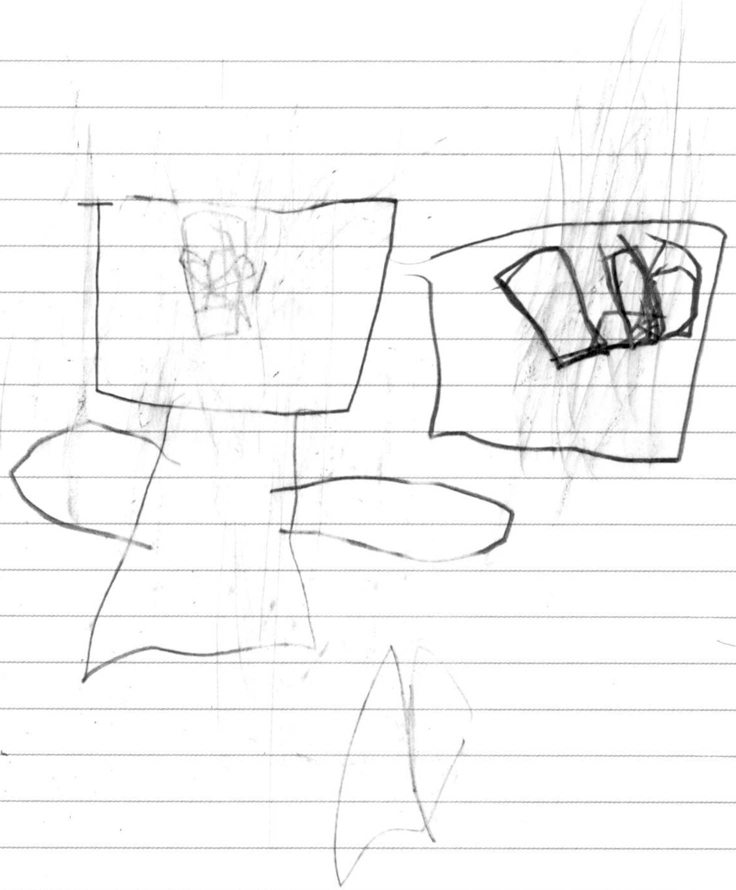

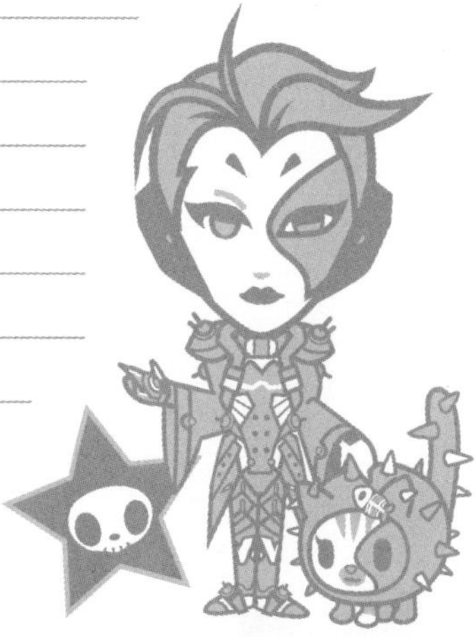

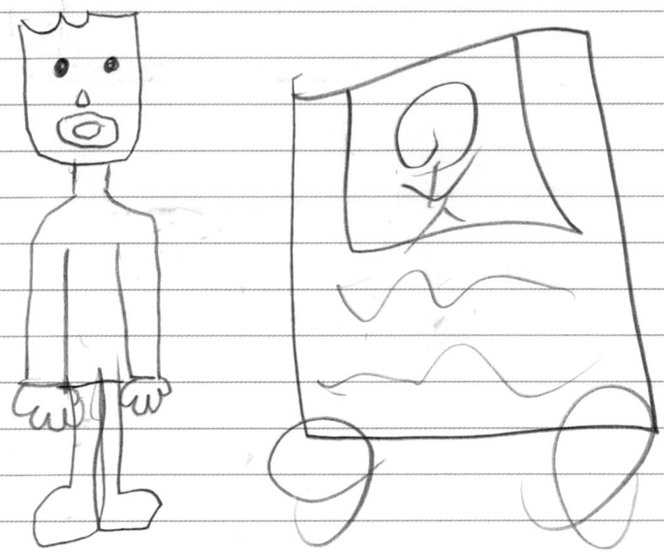

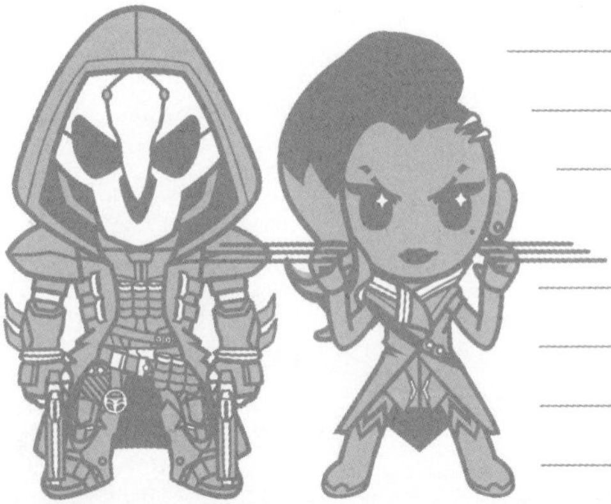

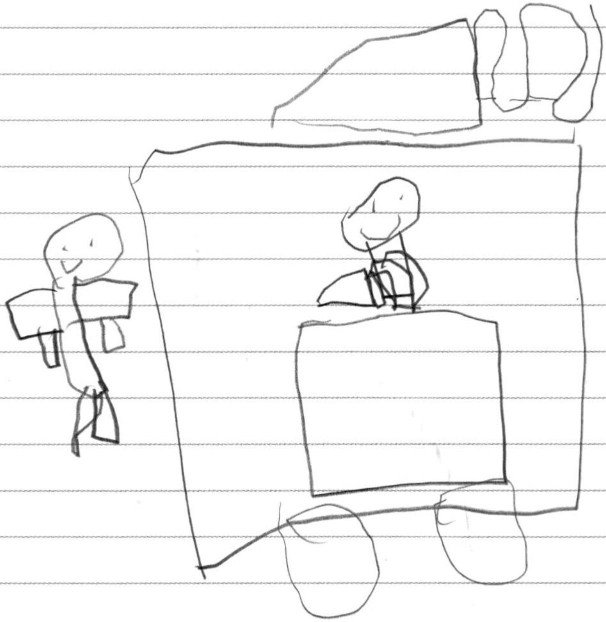

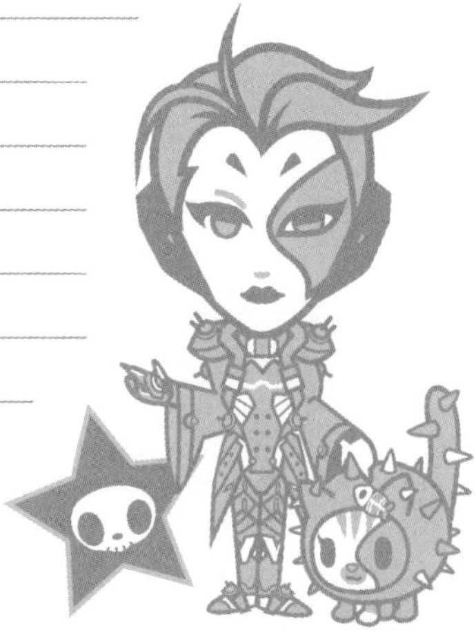

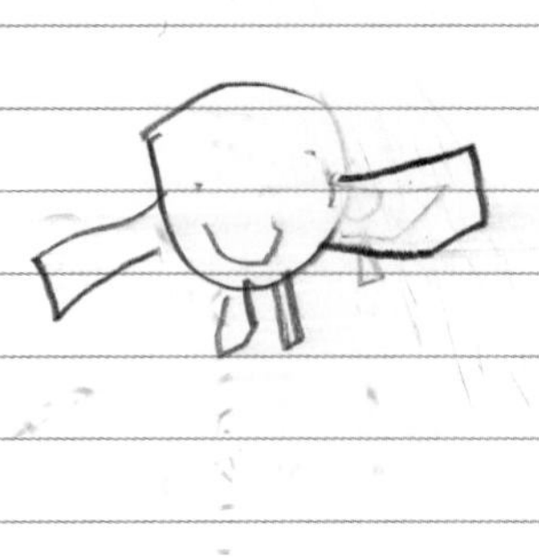

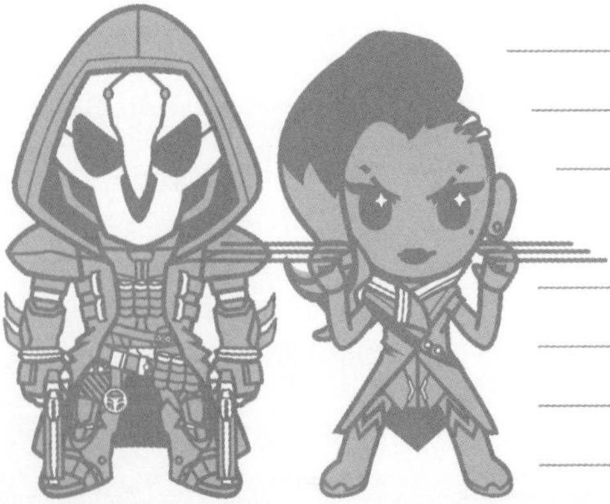

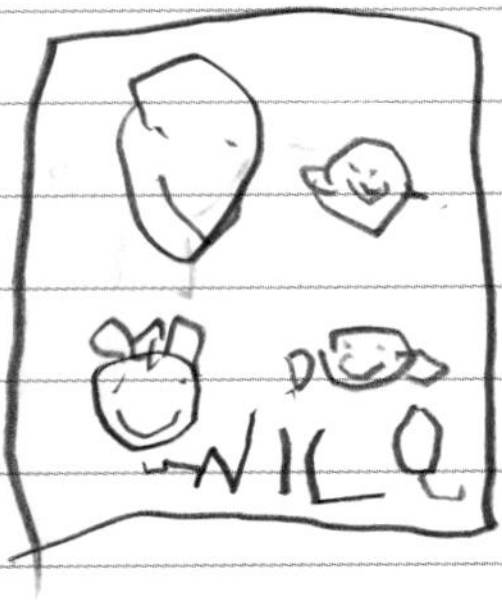

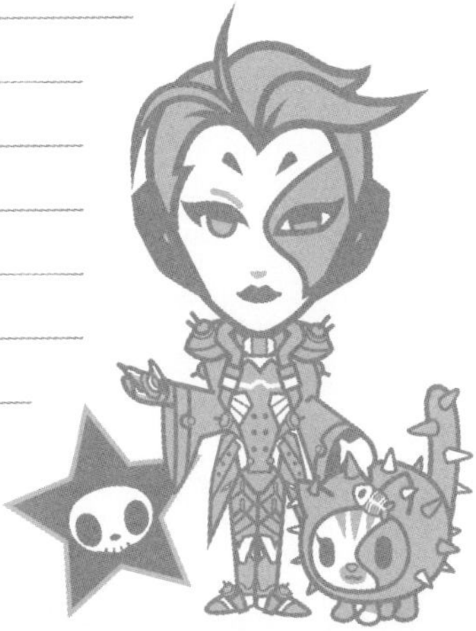

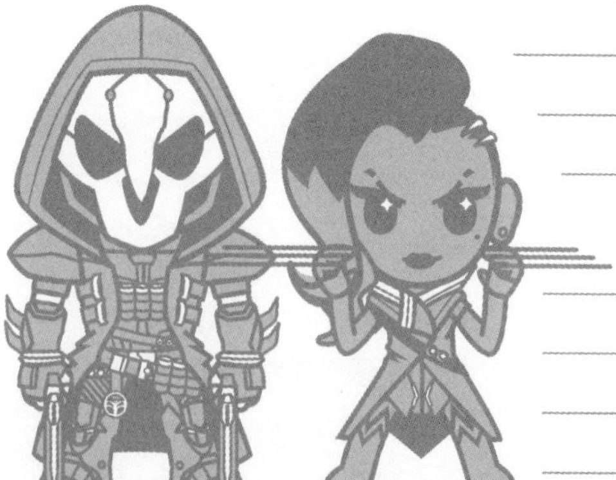

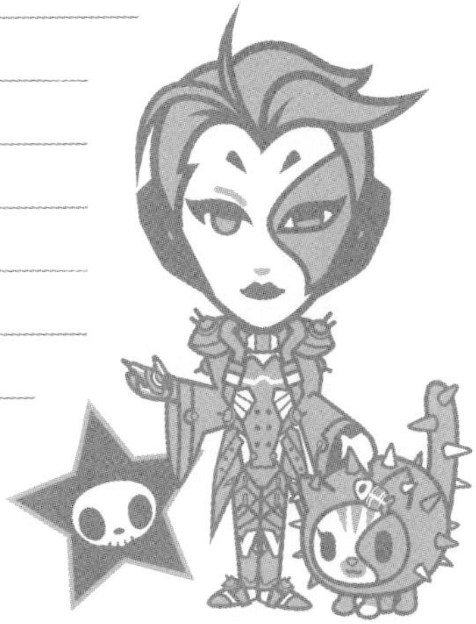

n 1 2 3 3 4 5 6

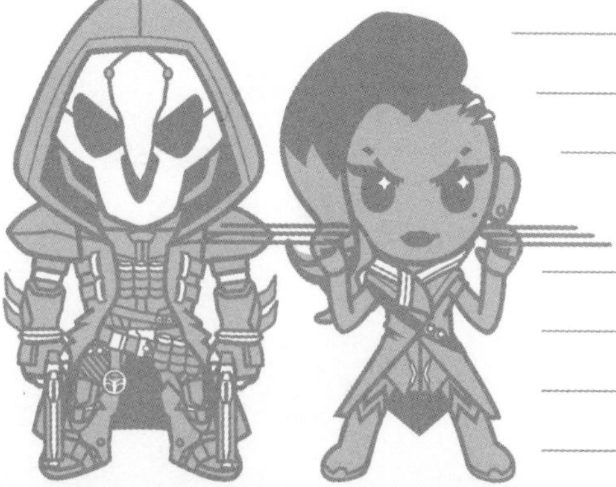

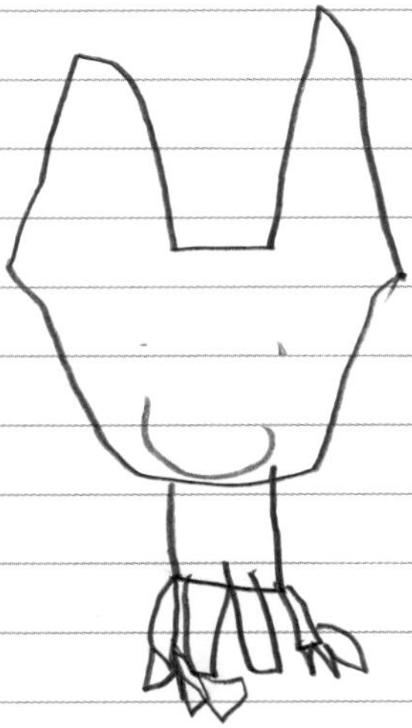

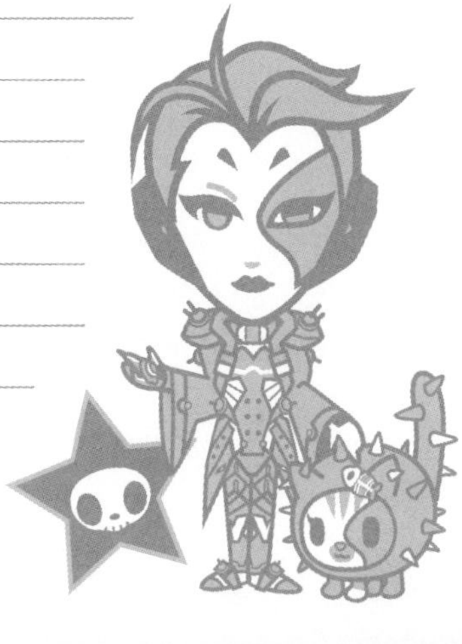

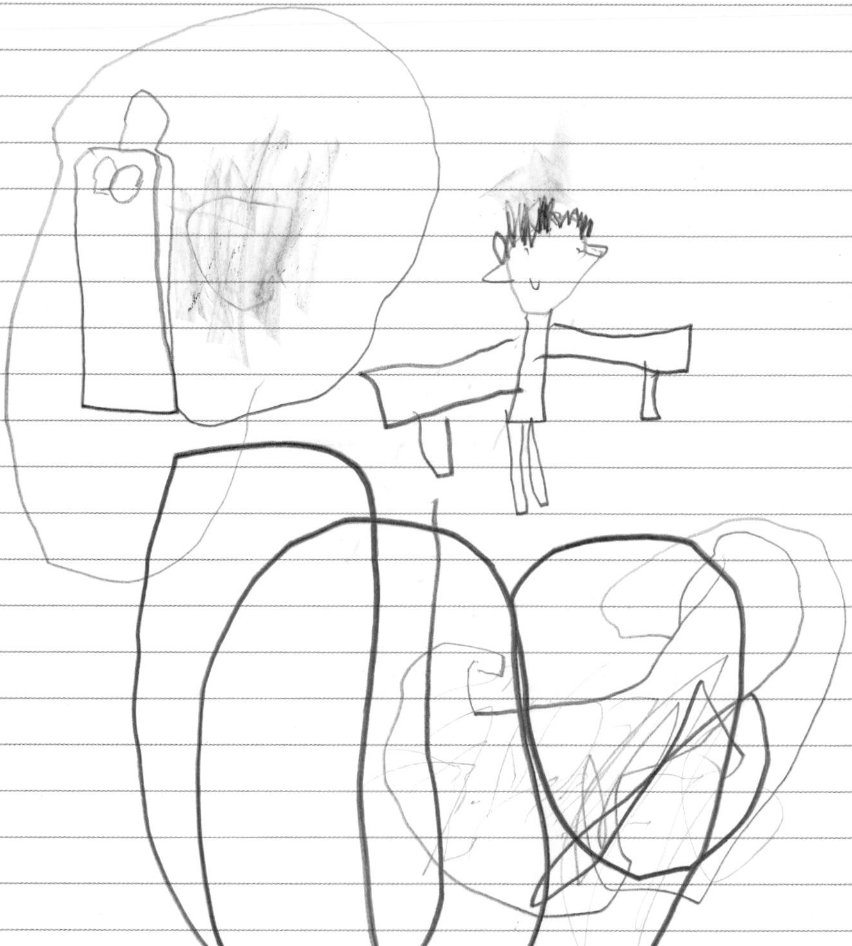

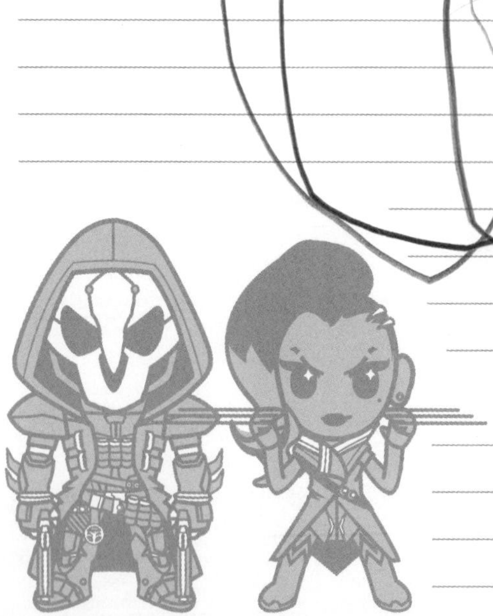

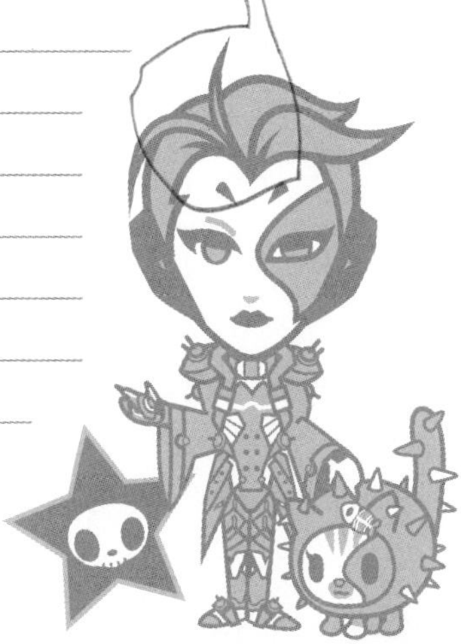

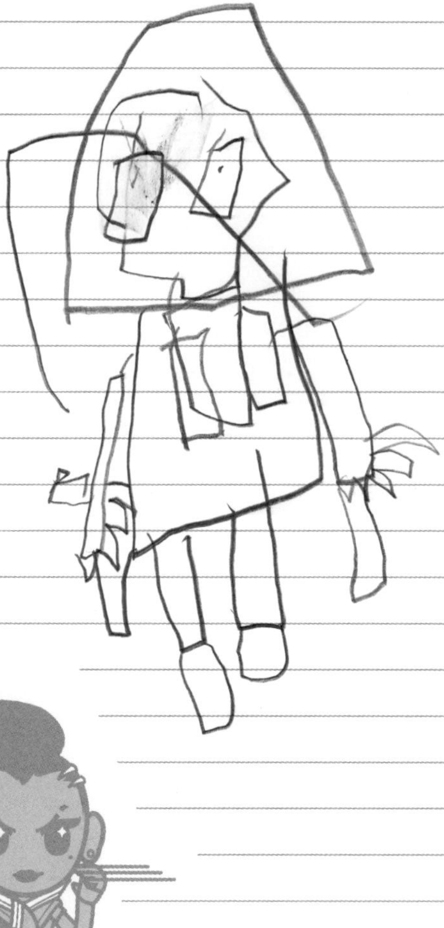

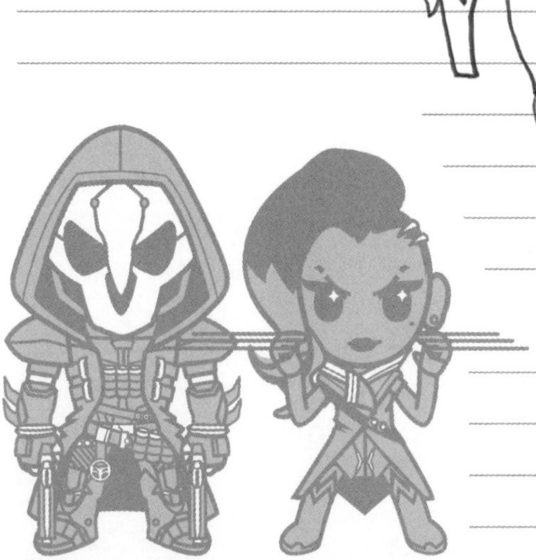

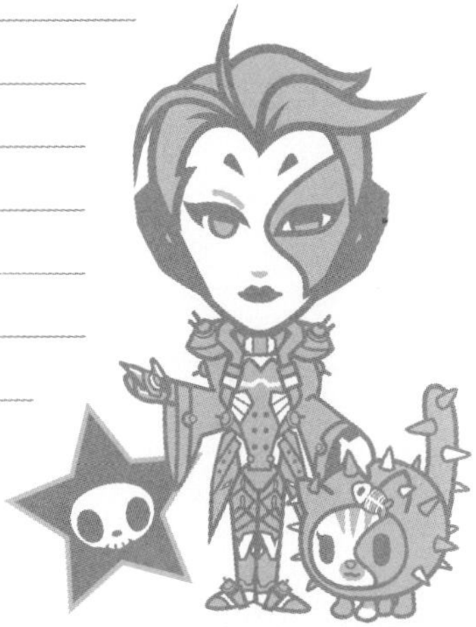

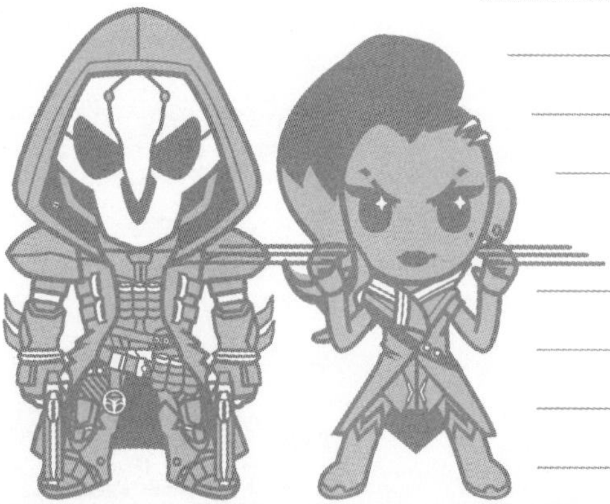

Cello Notes

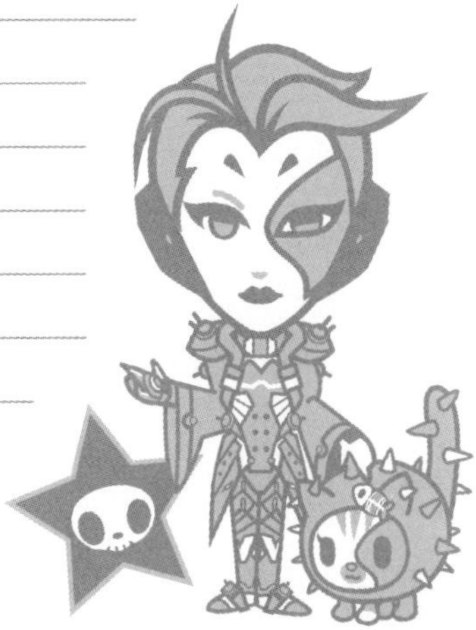

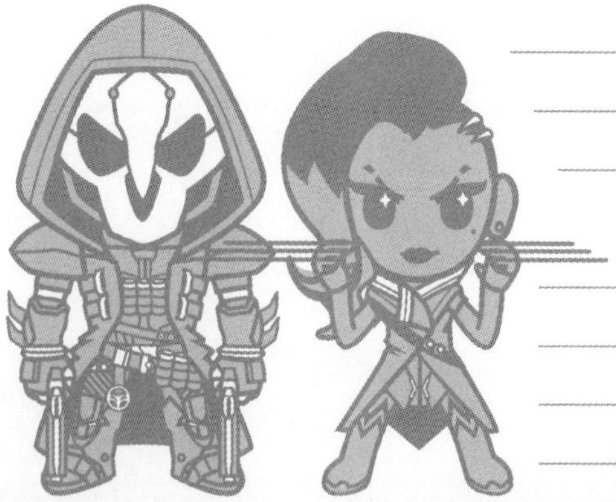

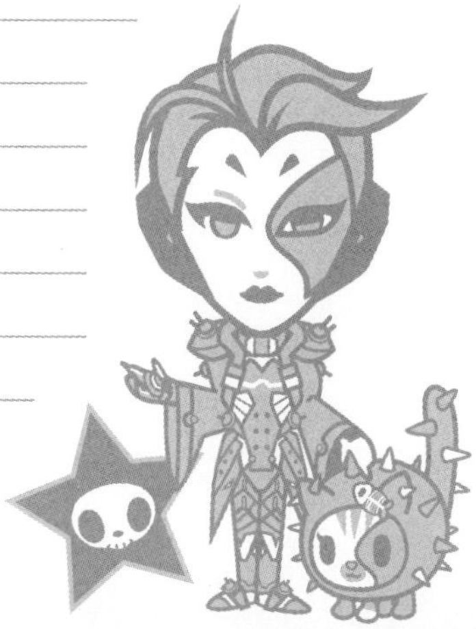

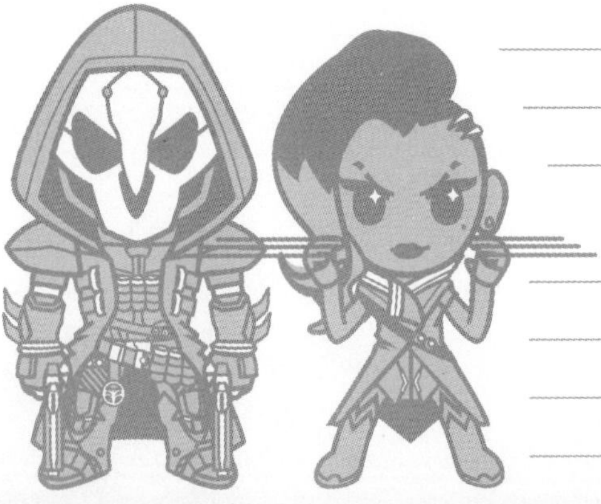

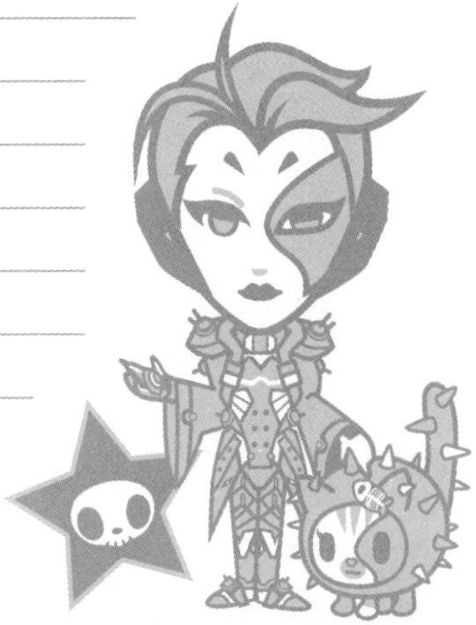

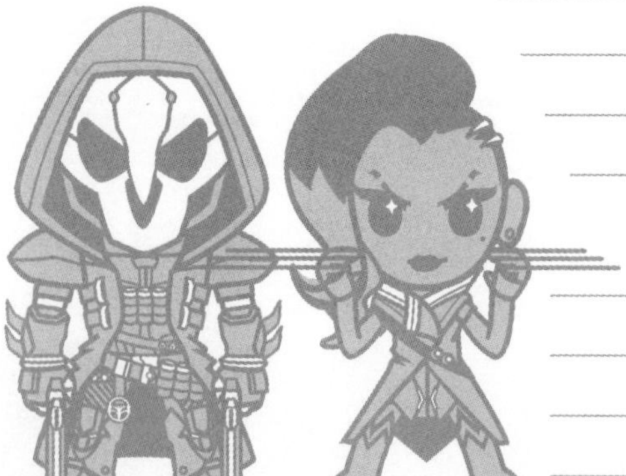

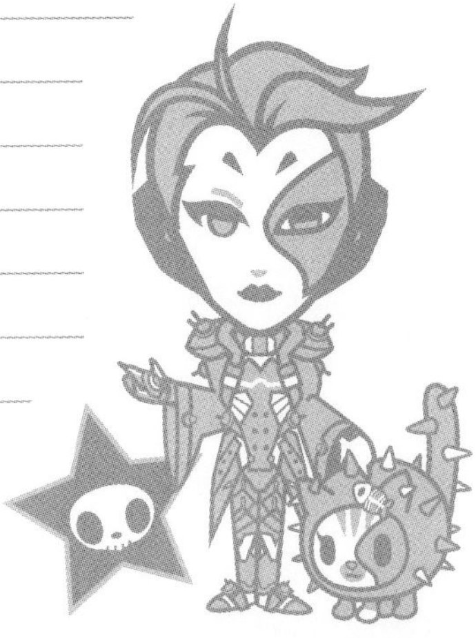

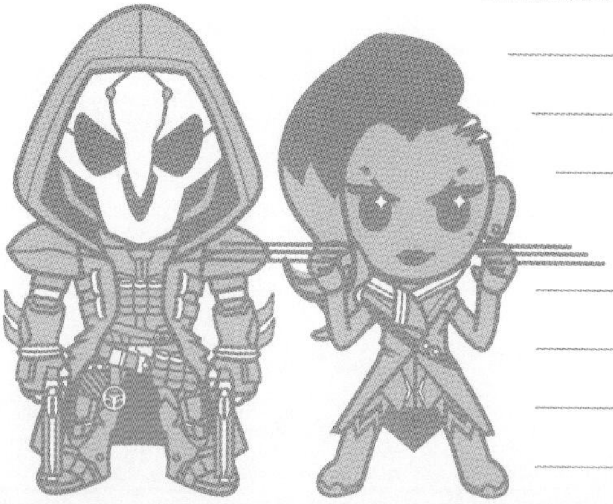

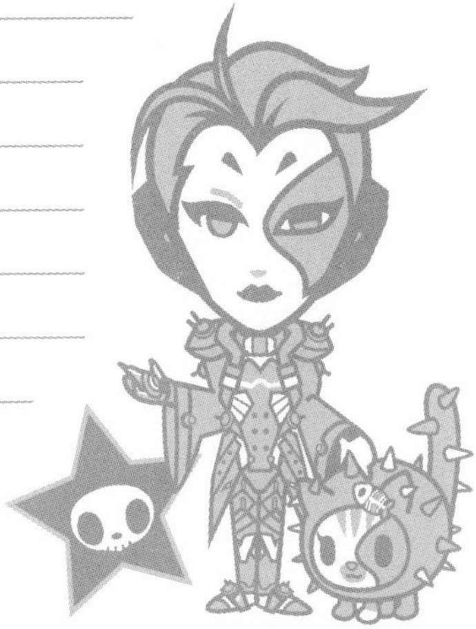

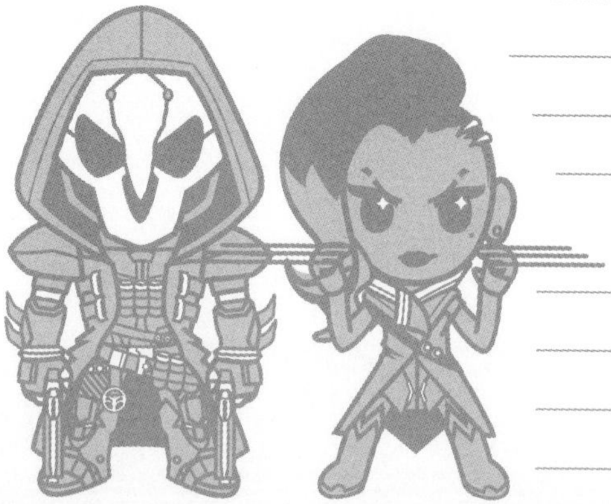

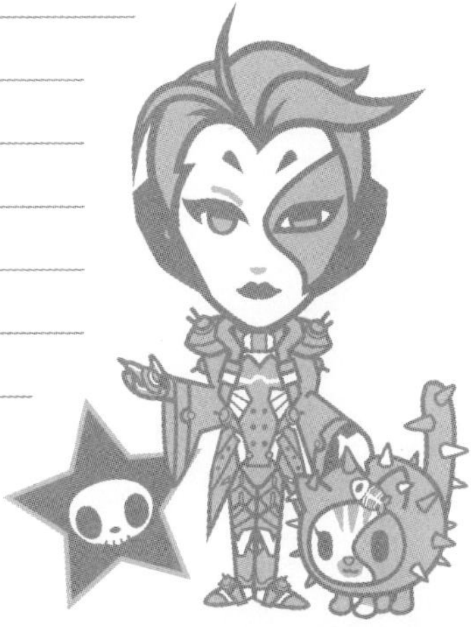

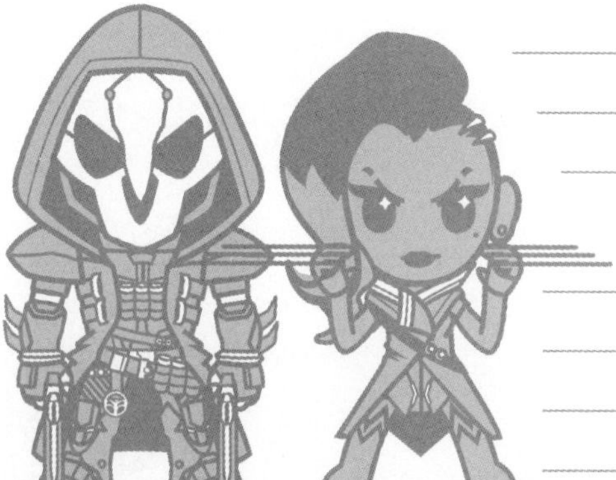

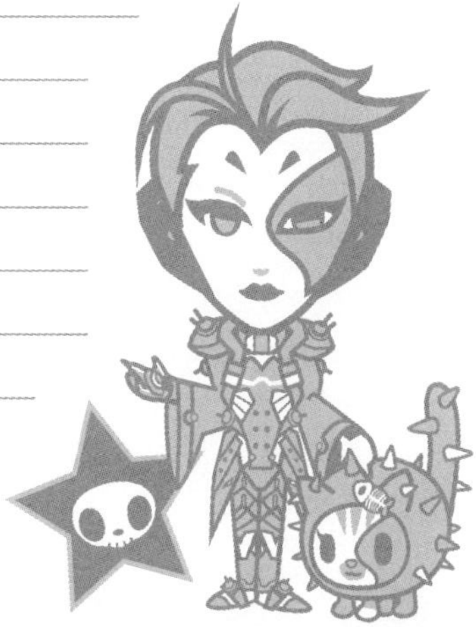

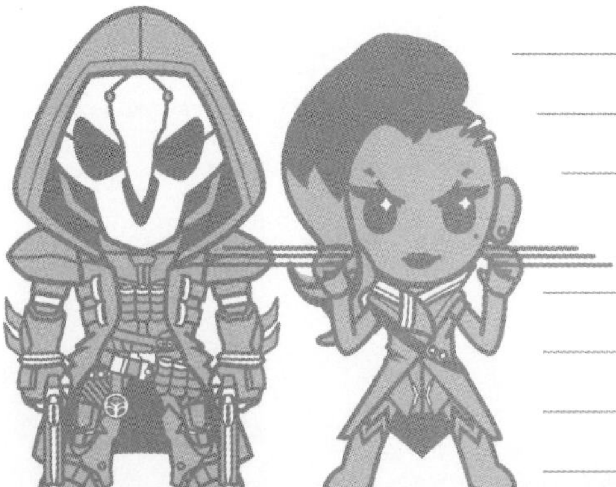

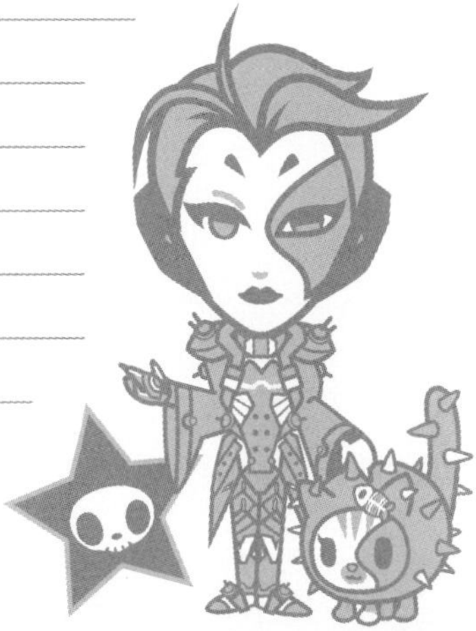

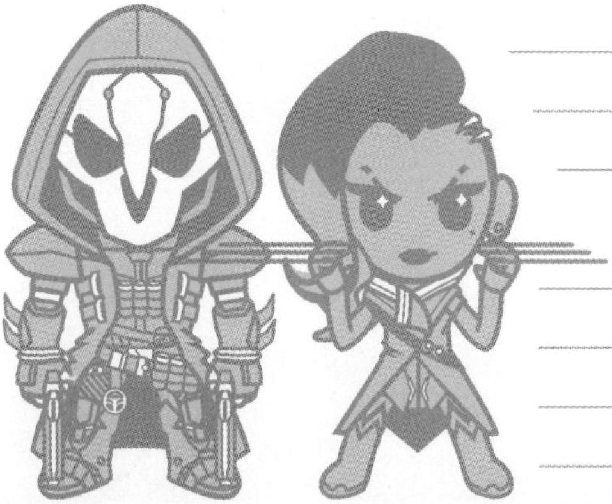

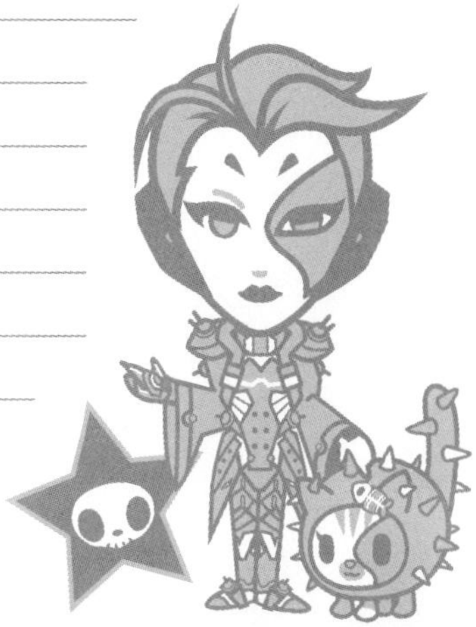

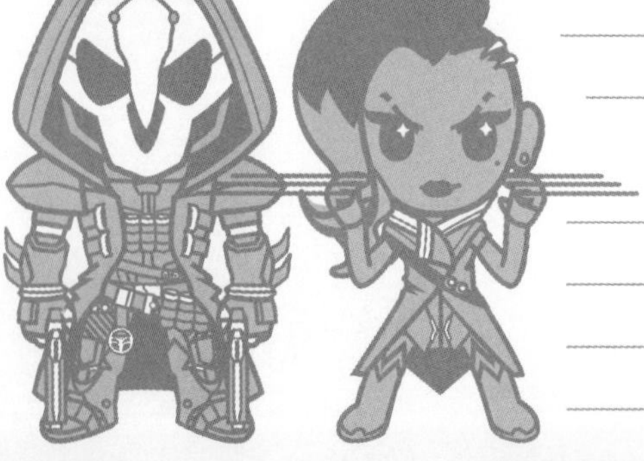

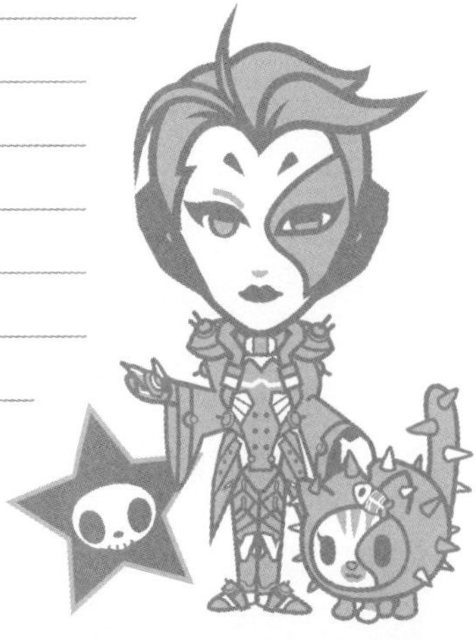

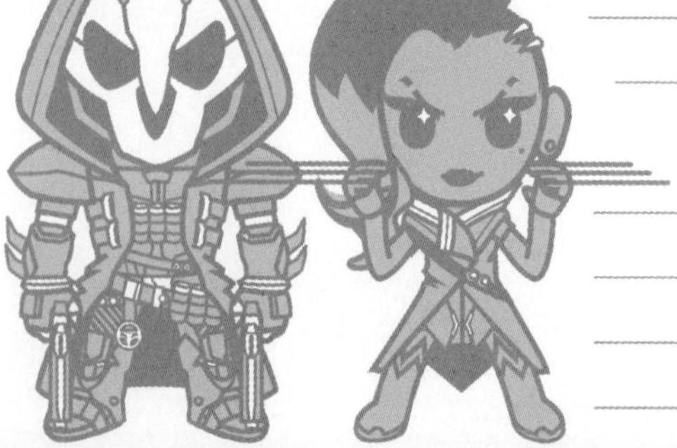

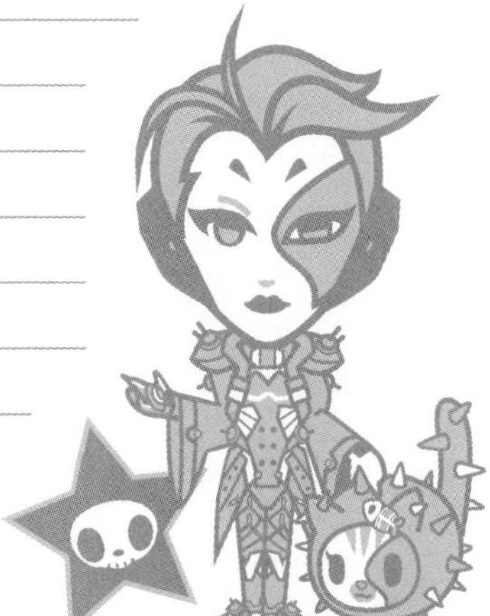

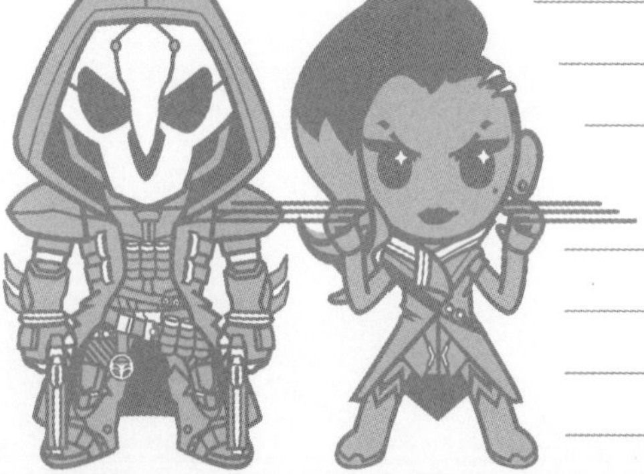

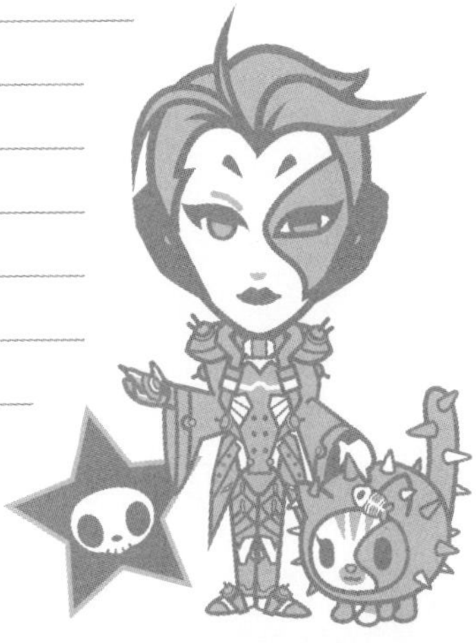

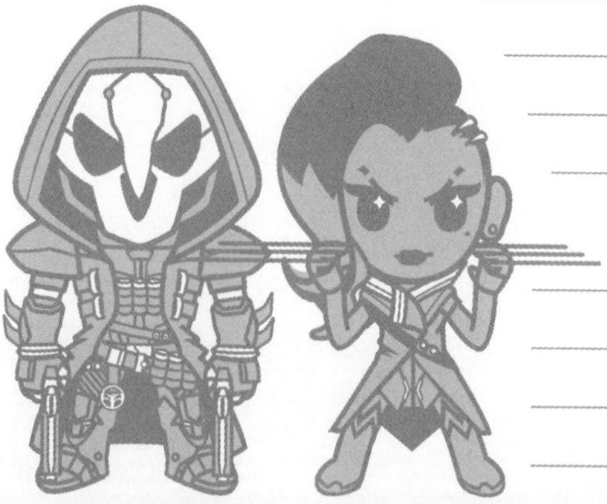

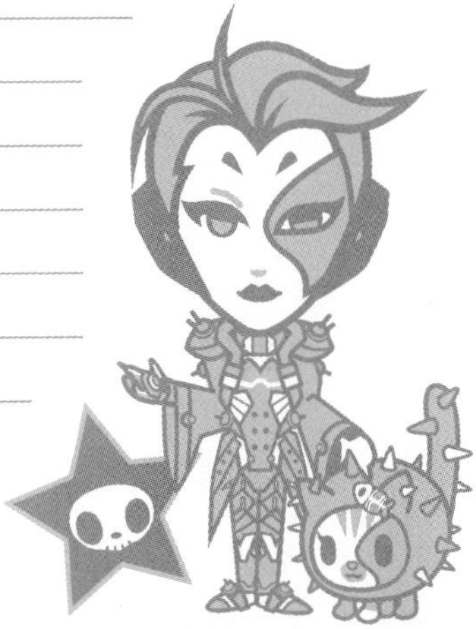

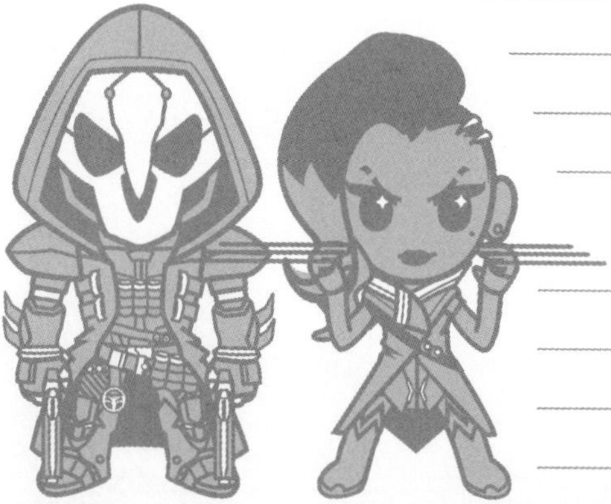

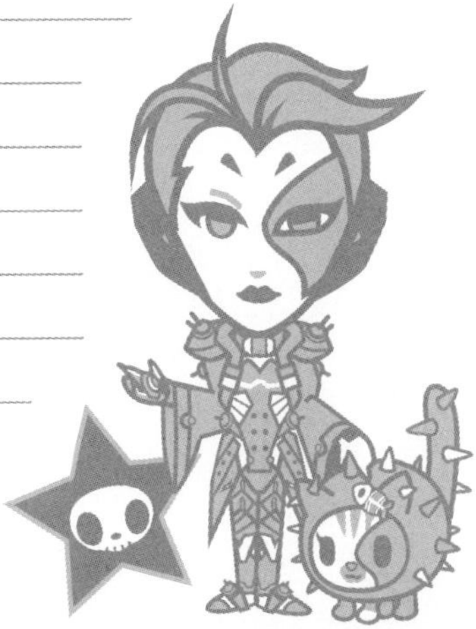

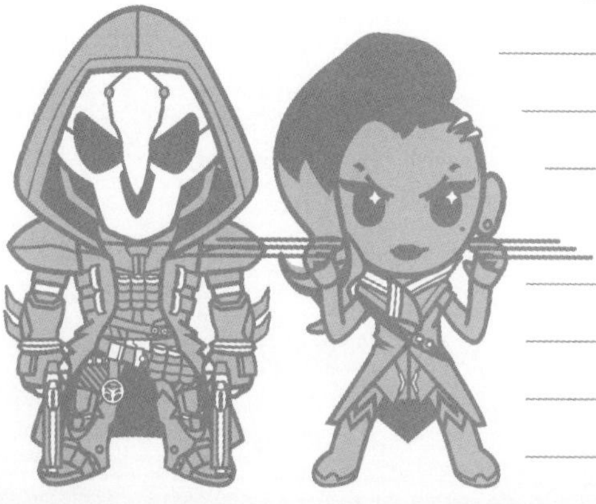

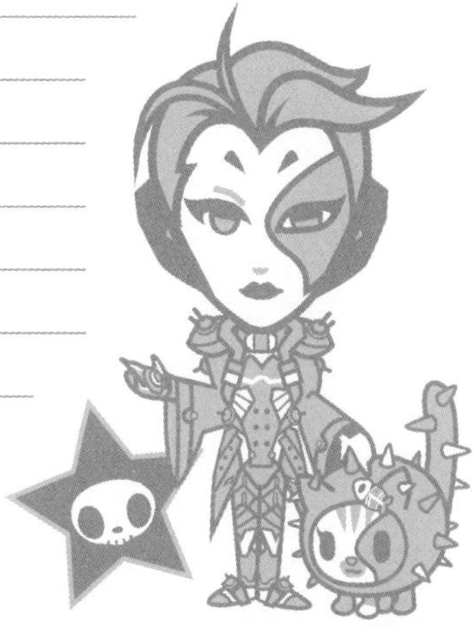

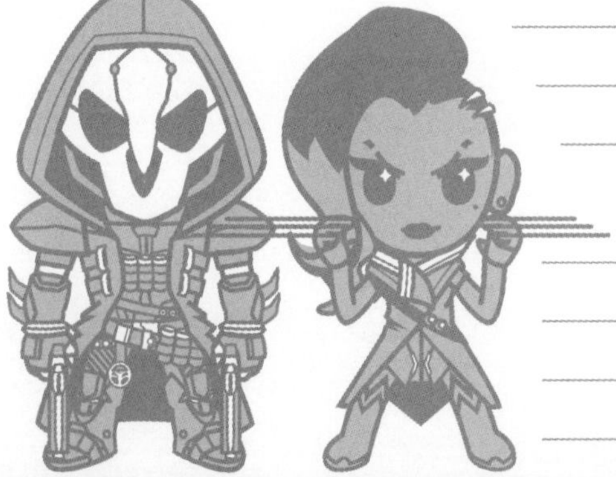

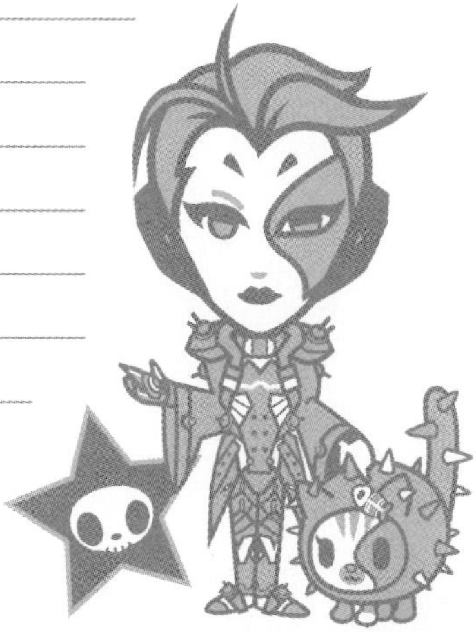

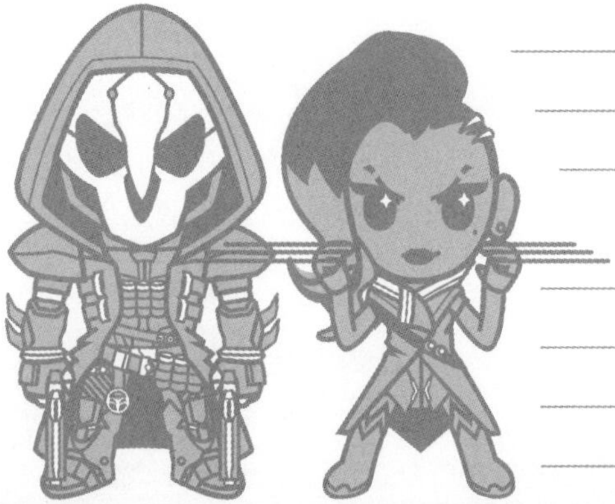

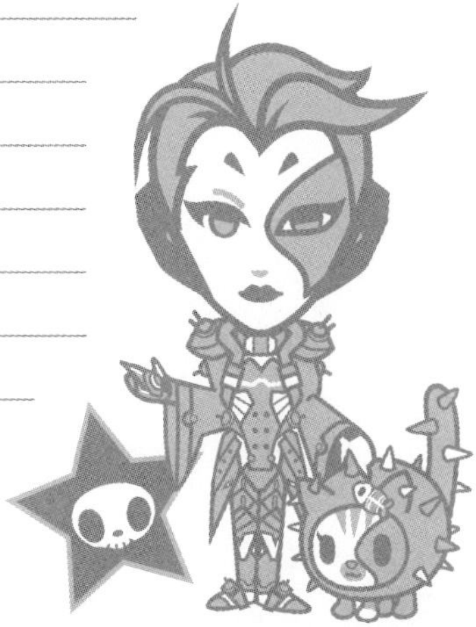

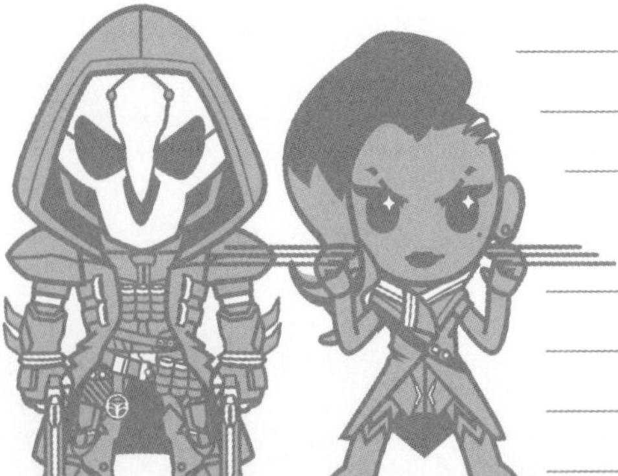

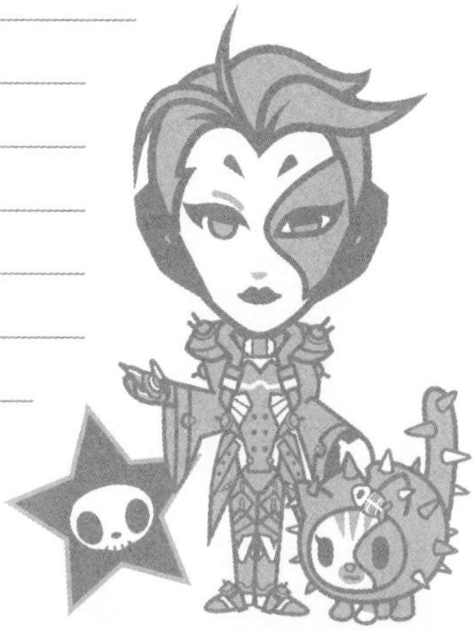

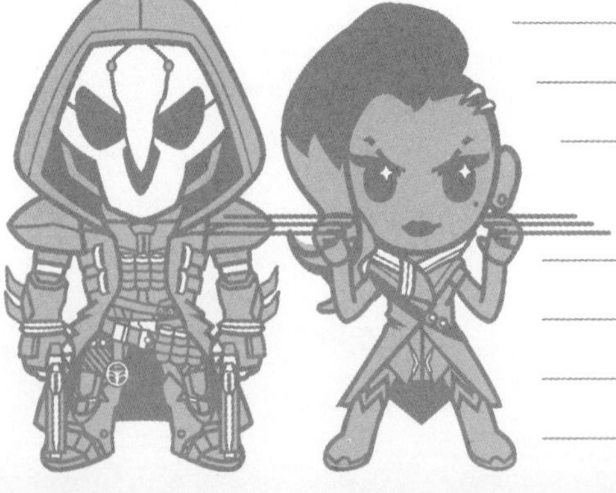

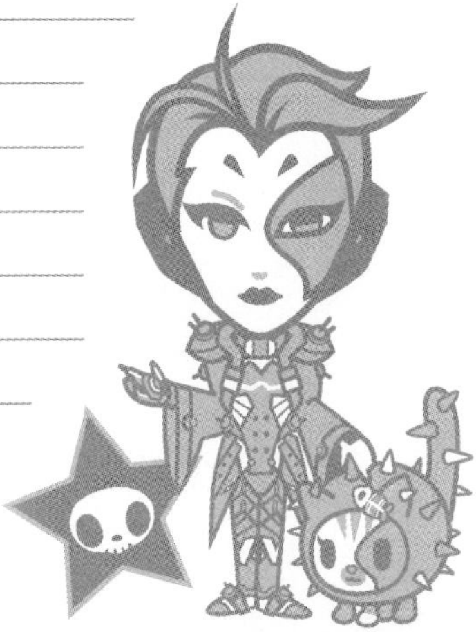

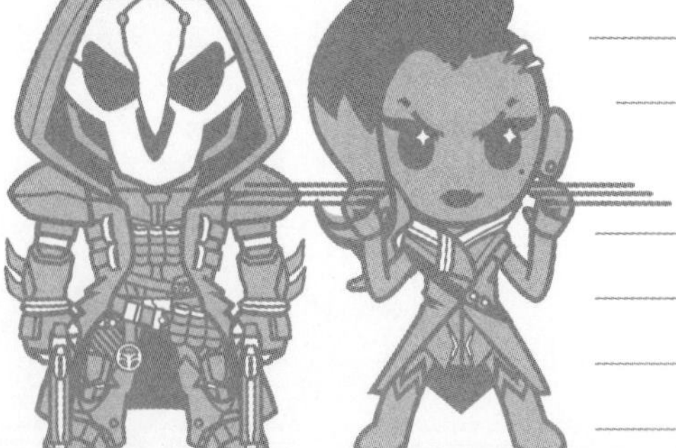

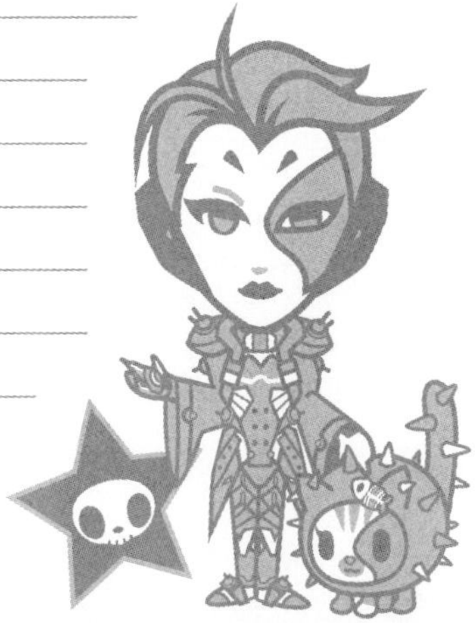

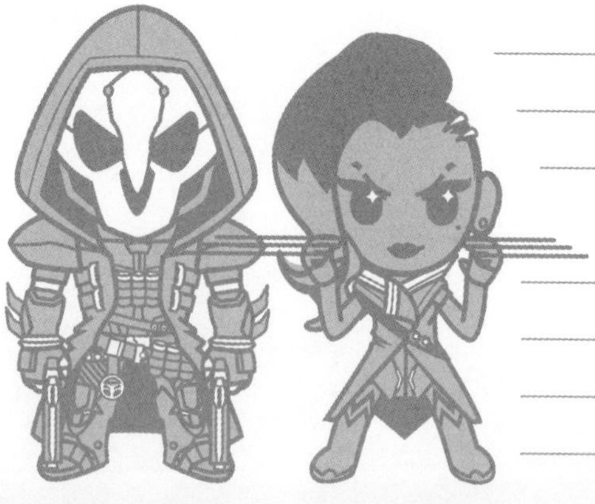

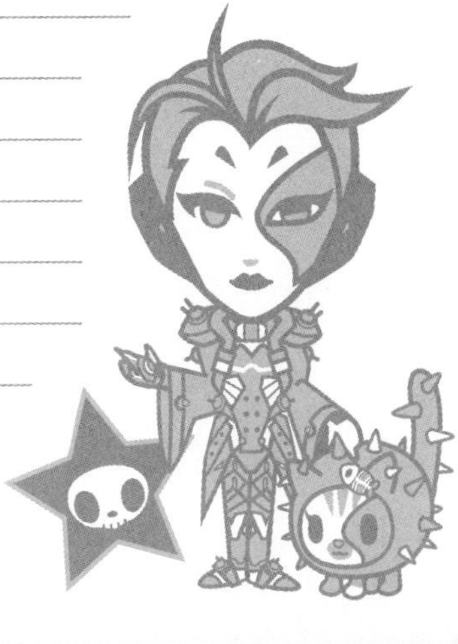

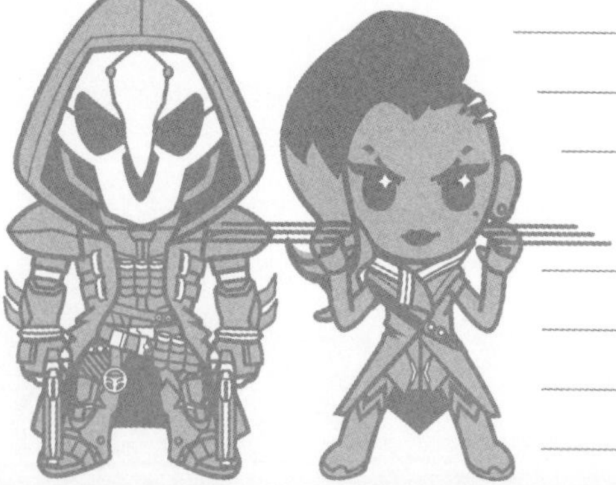

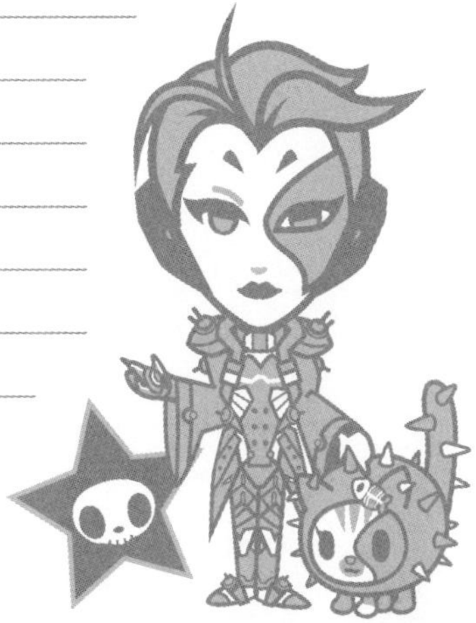

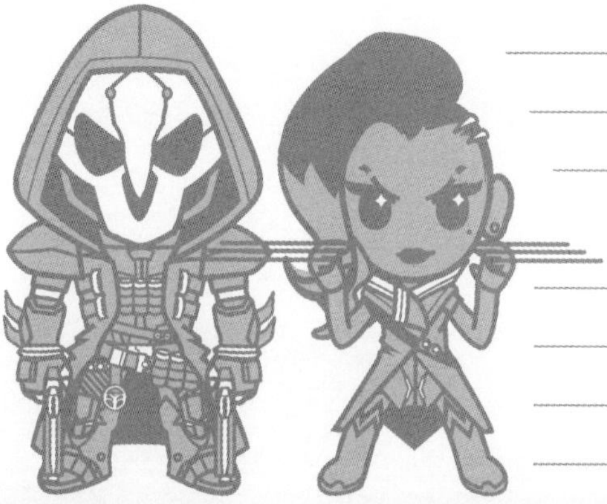

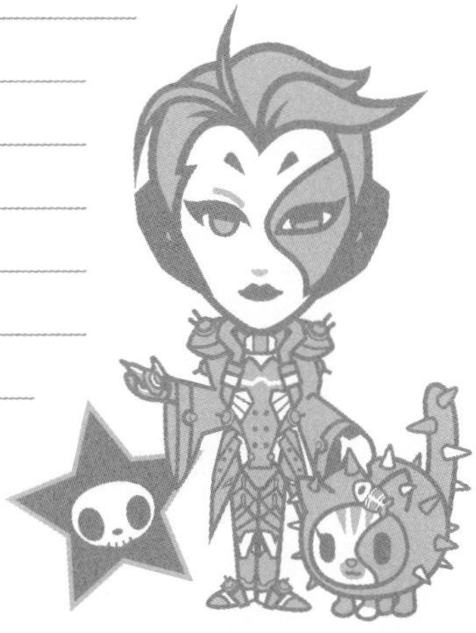

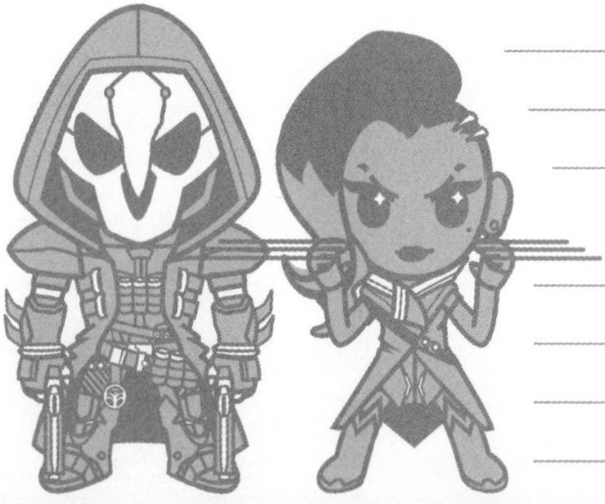

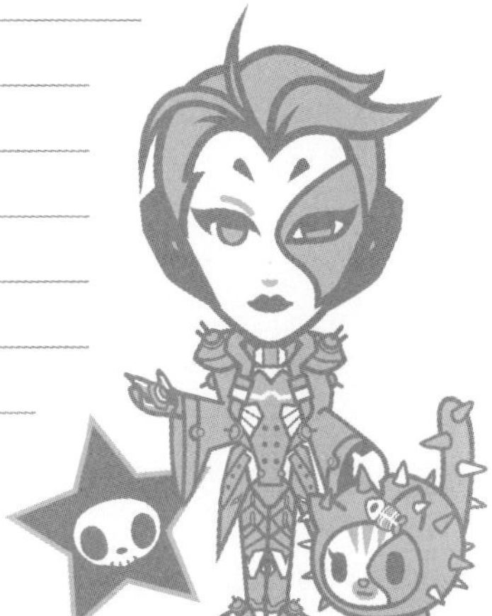

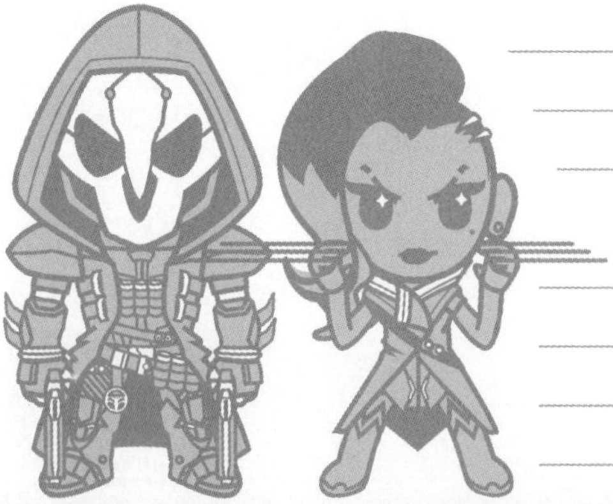

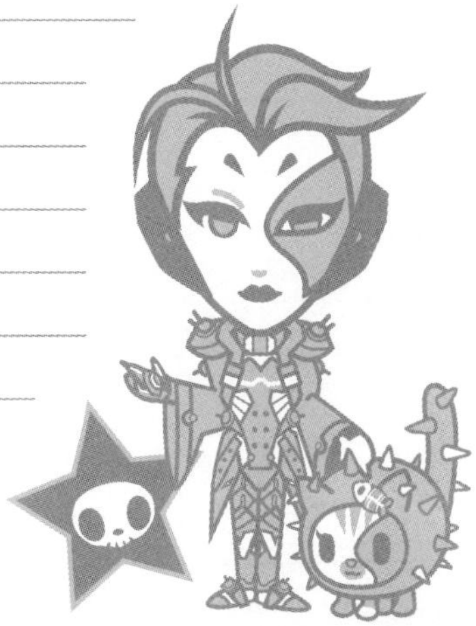

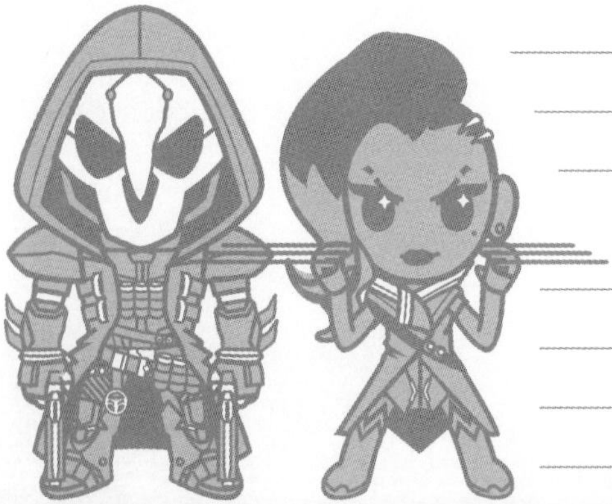

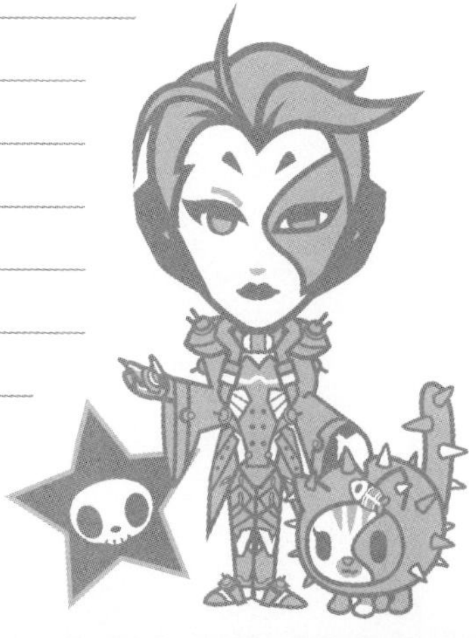

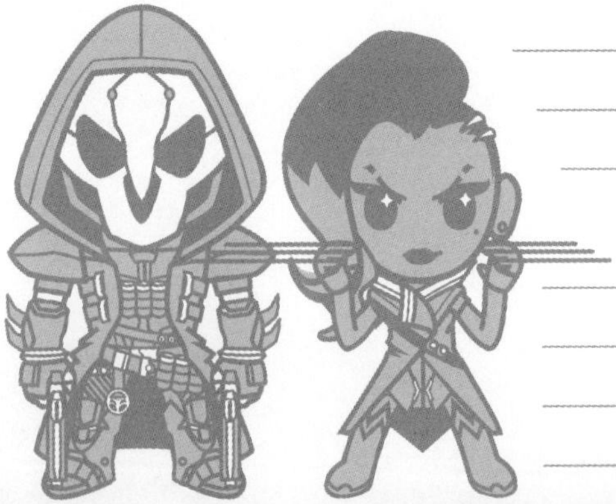

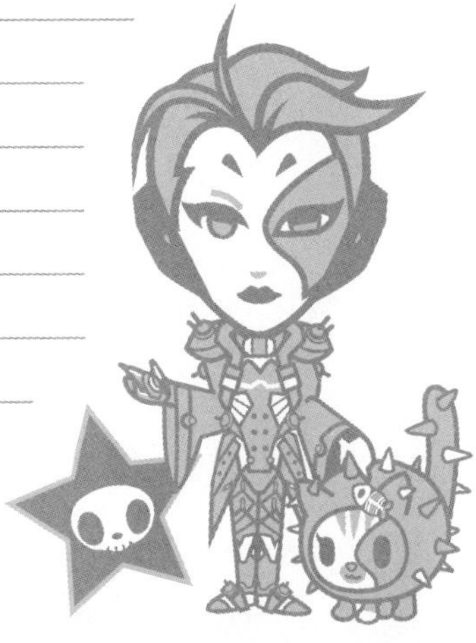

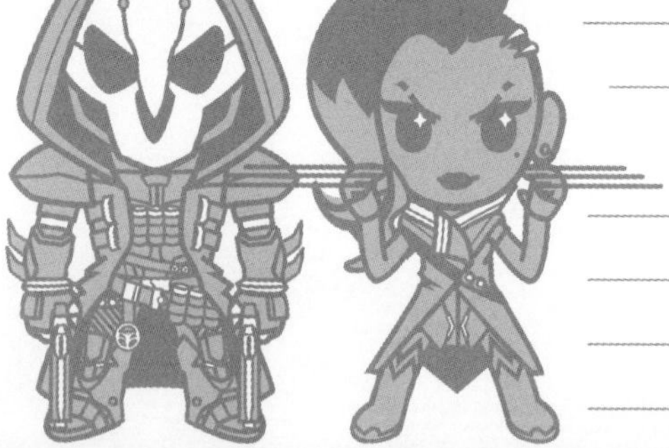

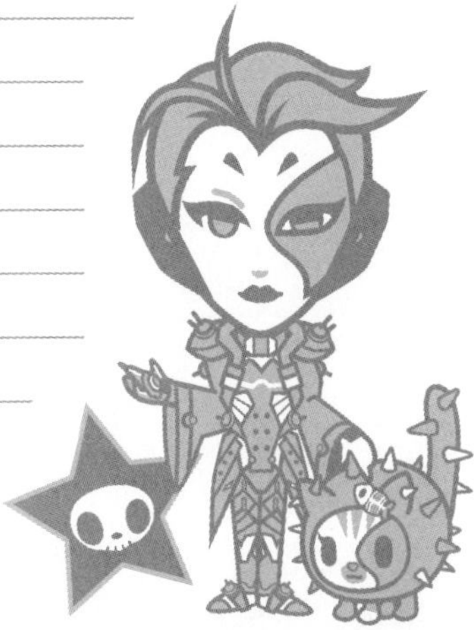

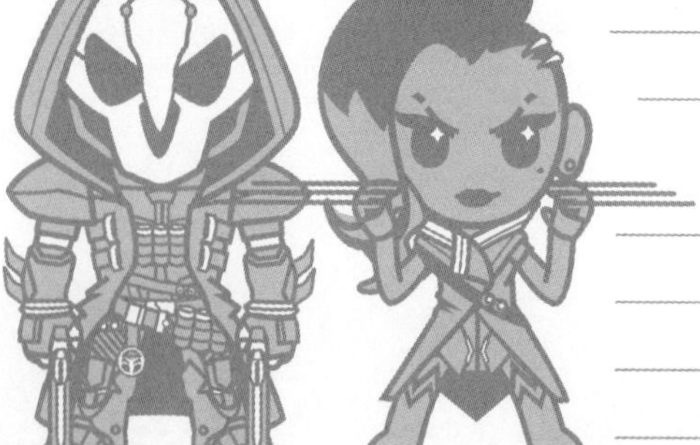

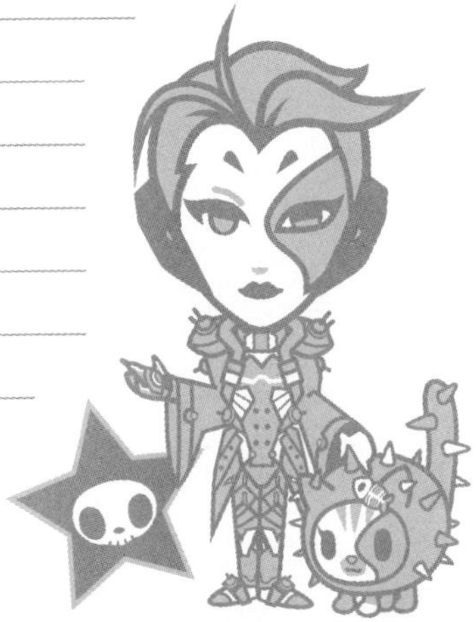

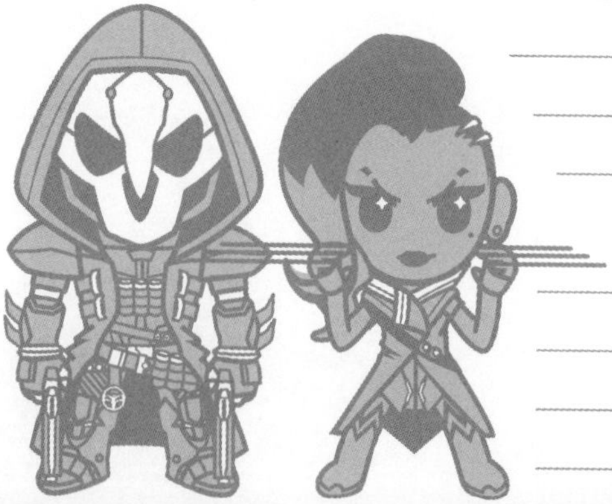

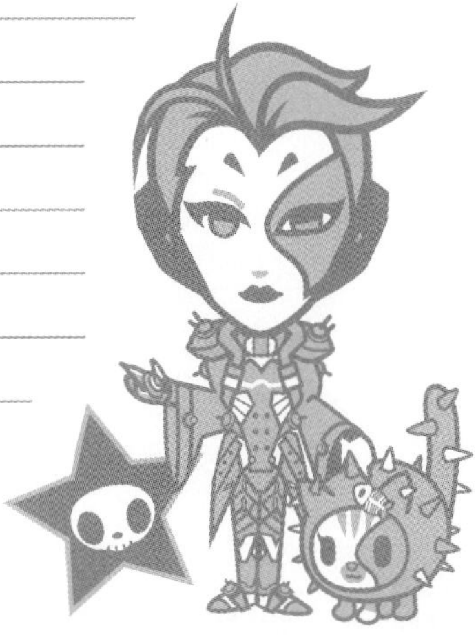

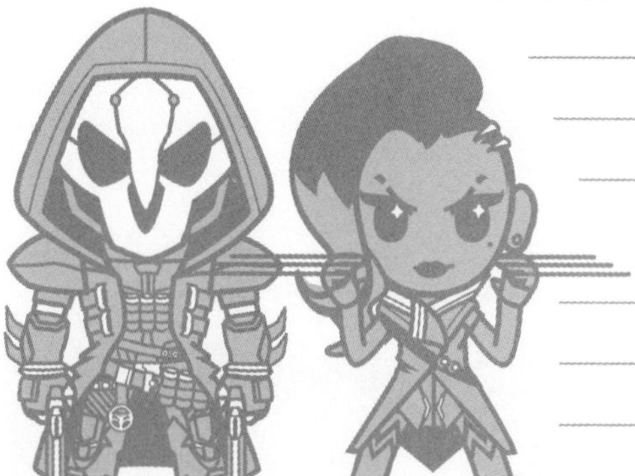

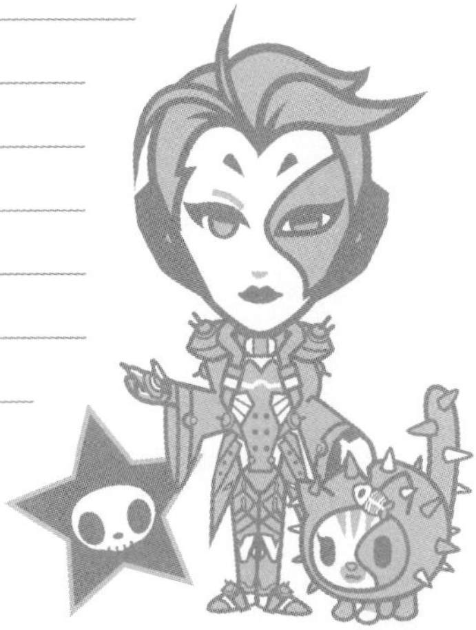

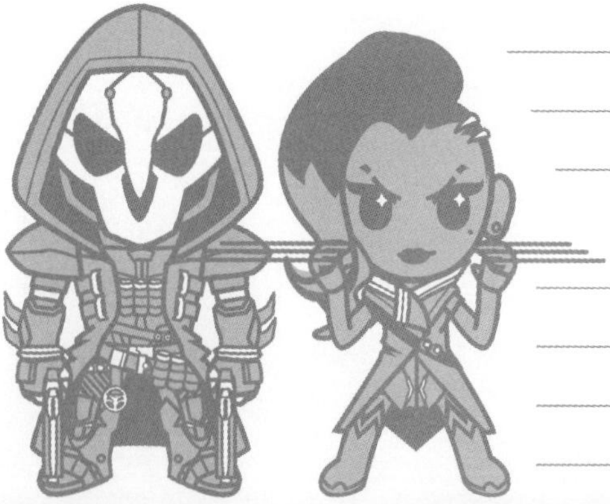

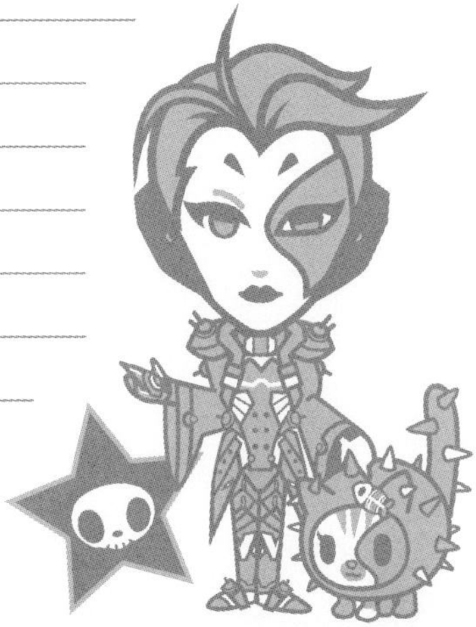

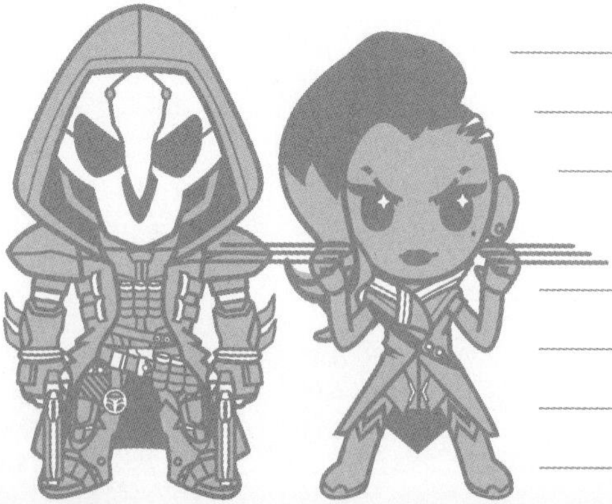

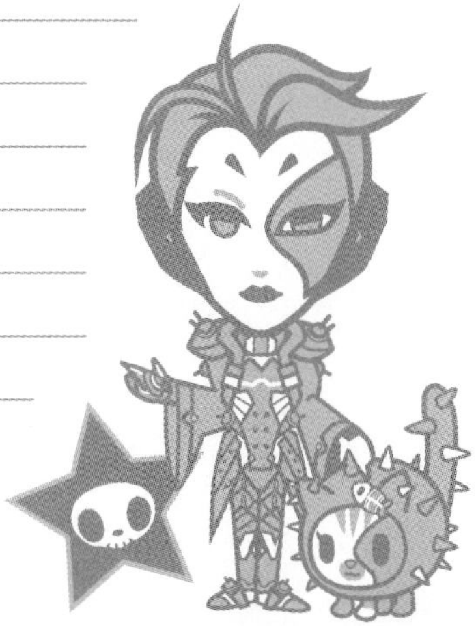

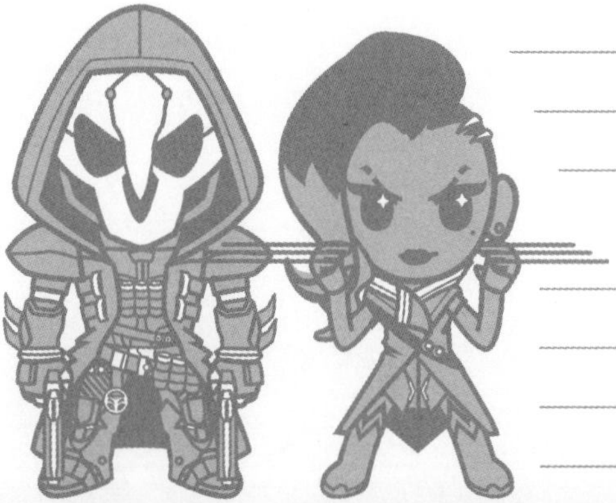

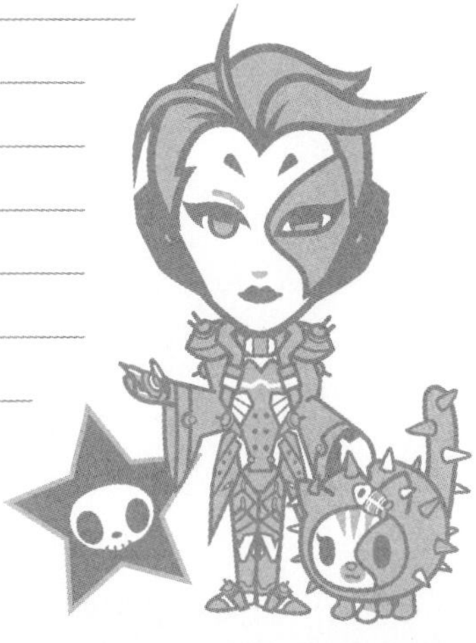

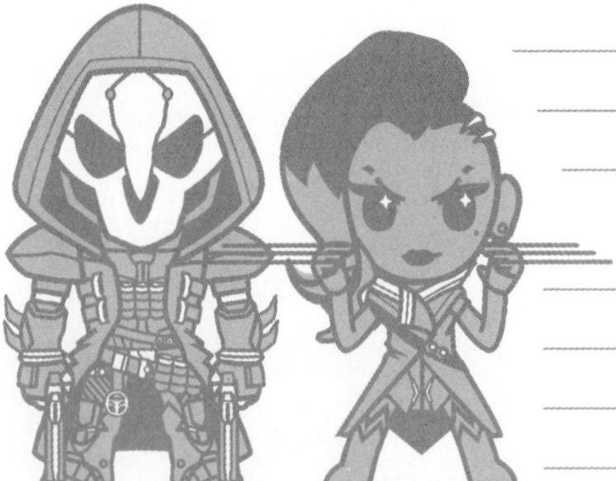

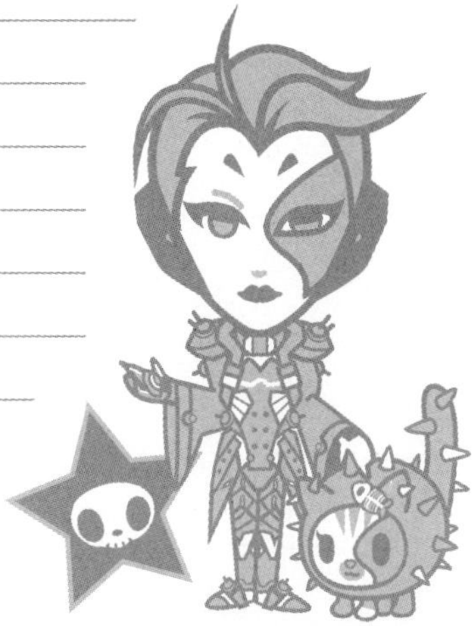

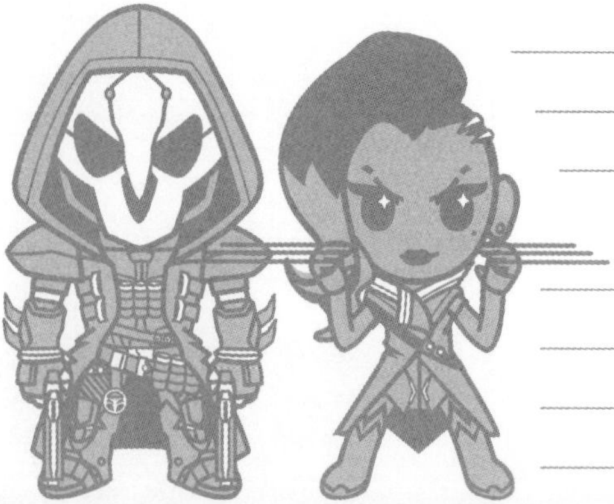

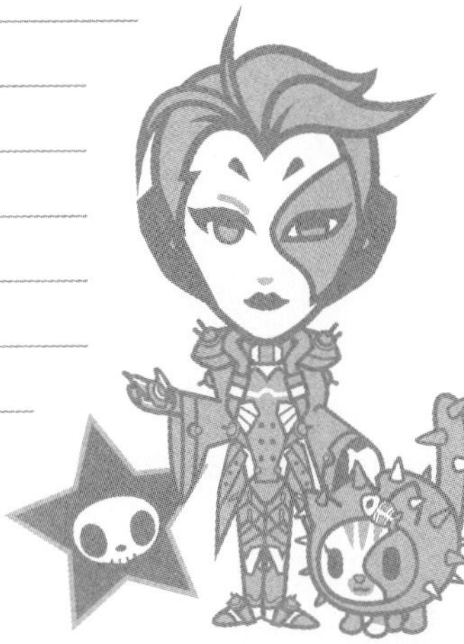

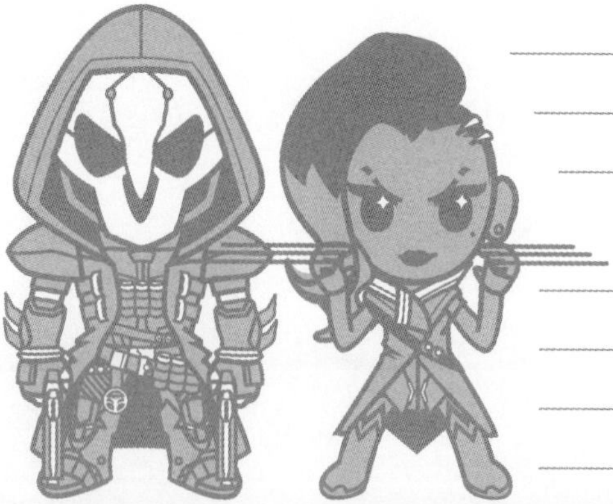

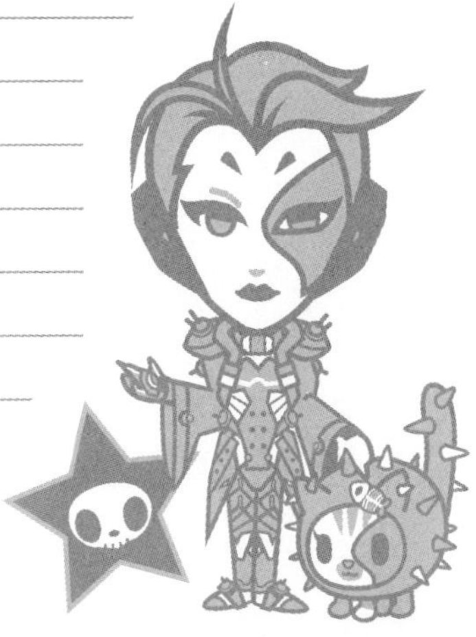

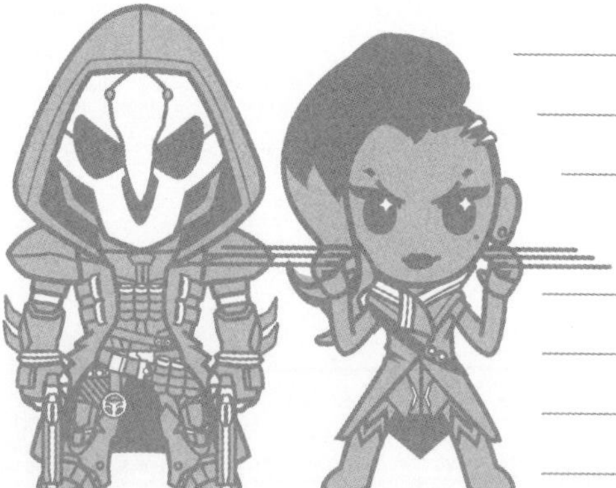

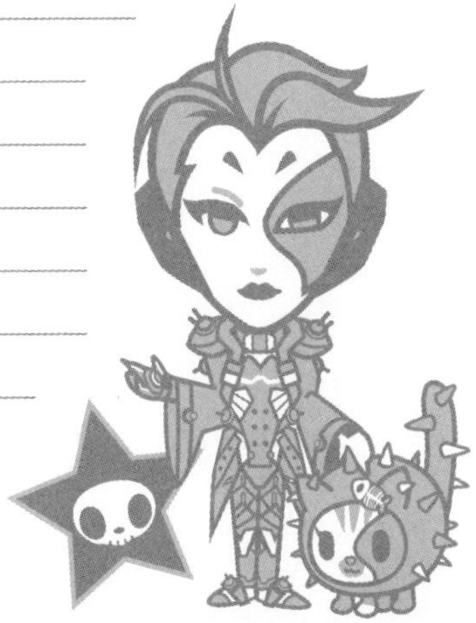

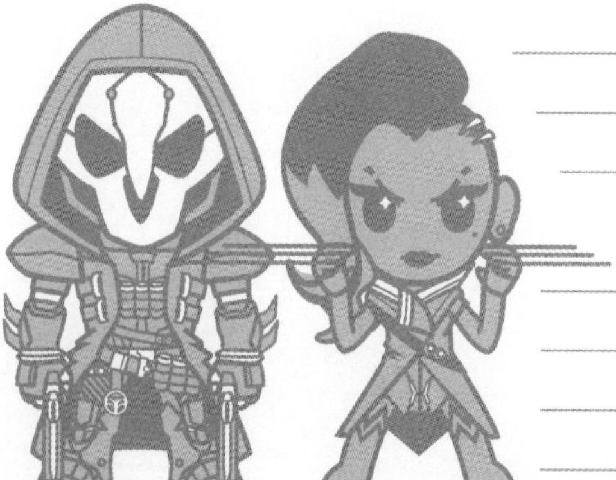

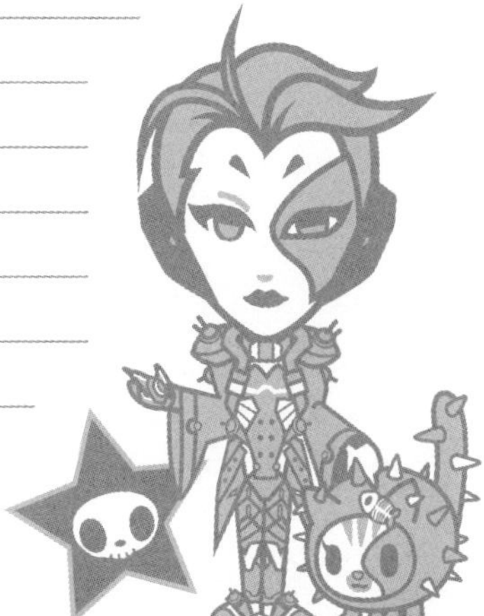

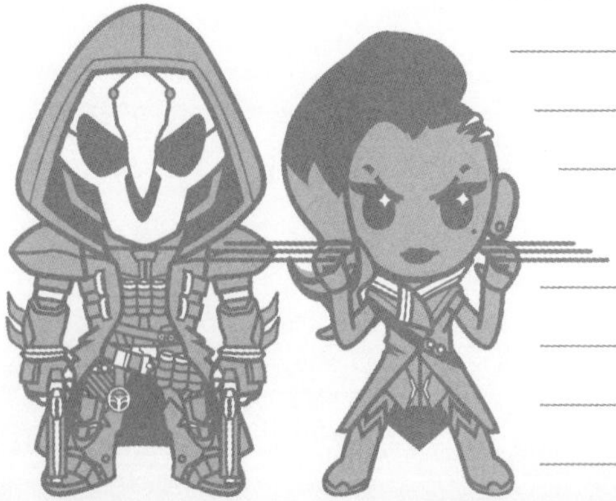

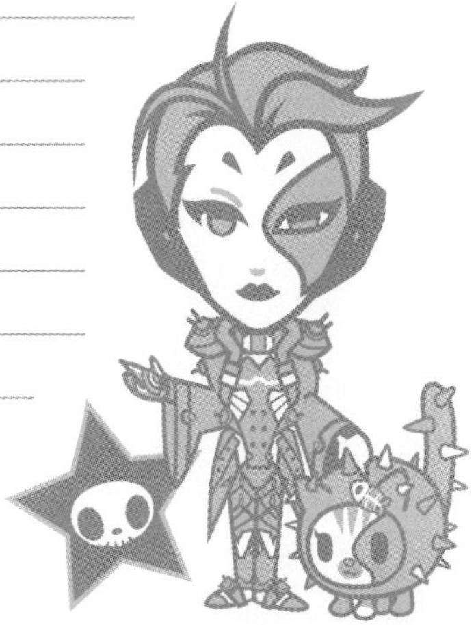

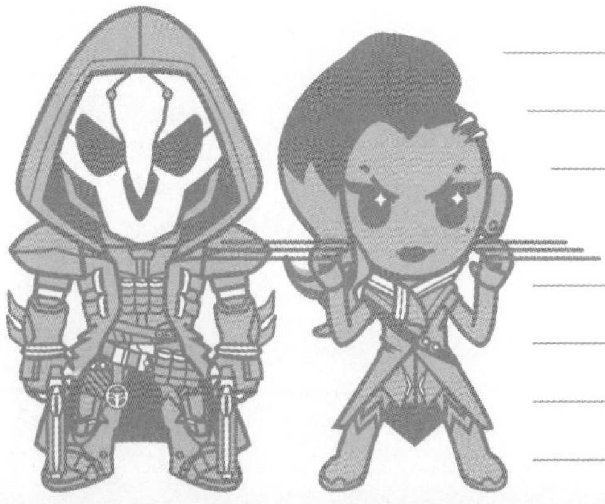

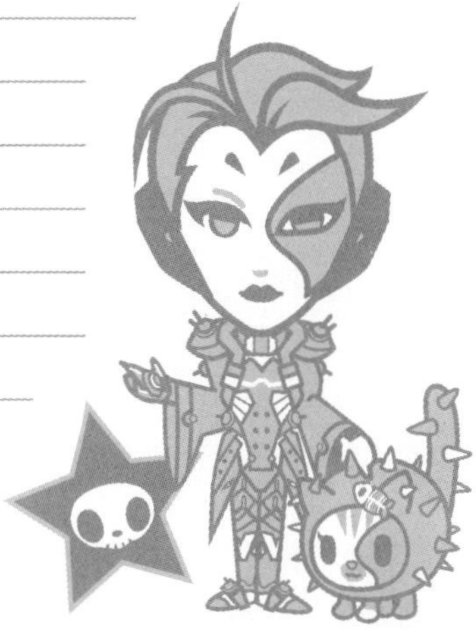

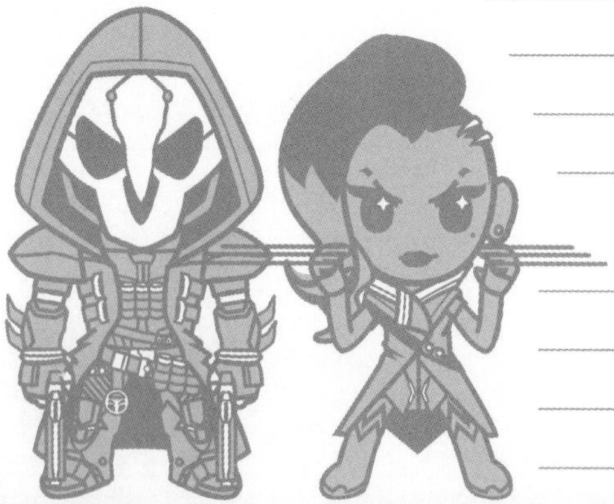

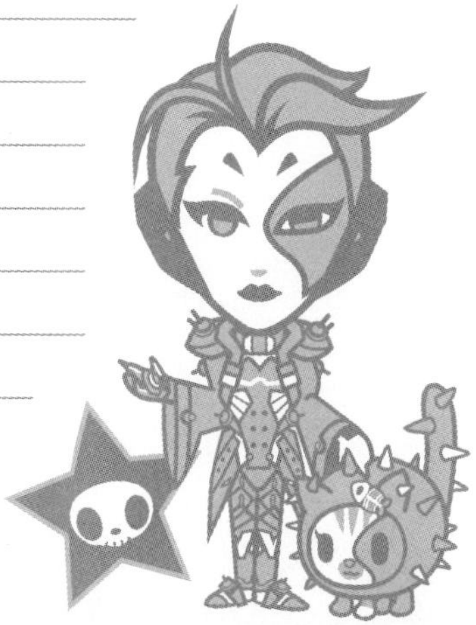

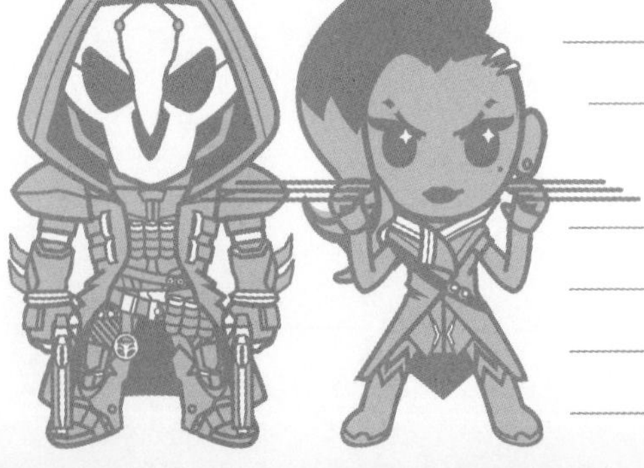

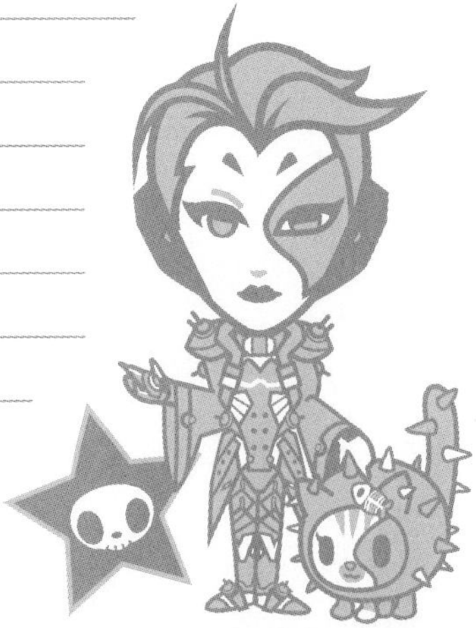

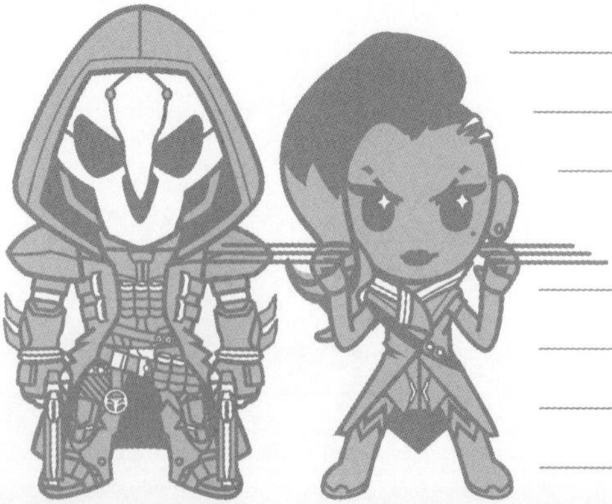

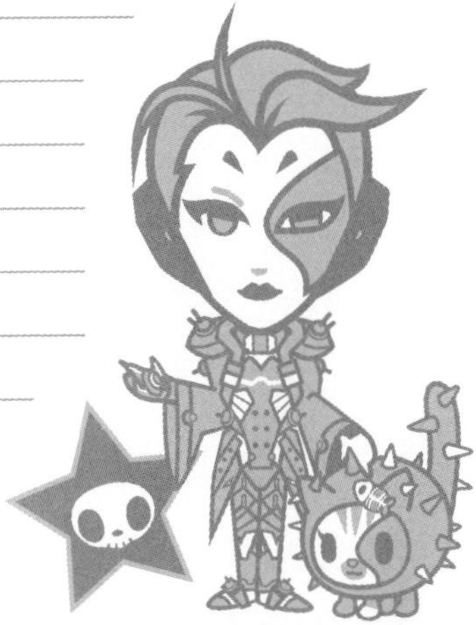

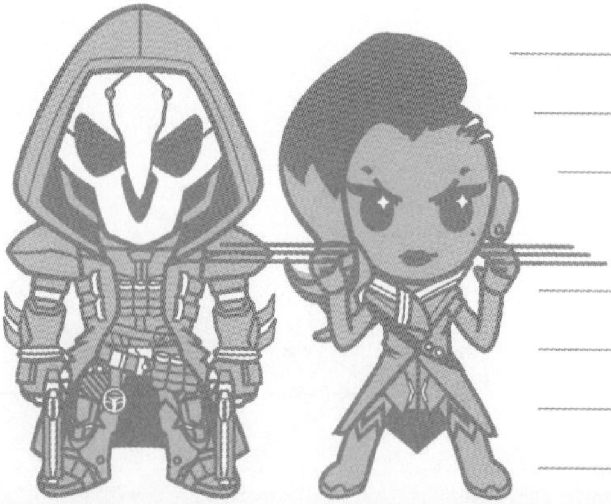

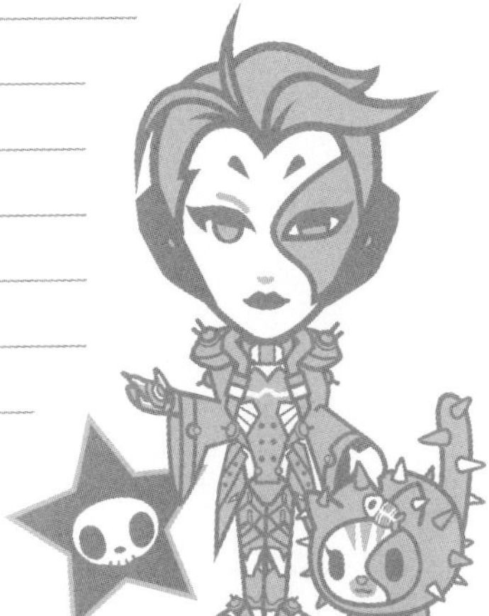

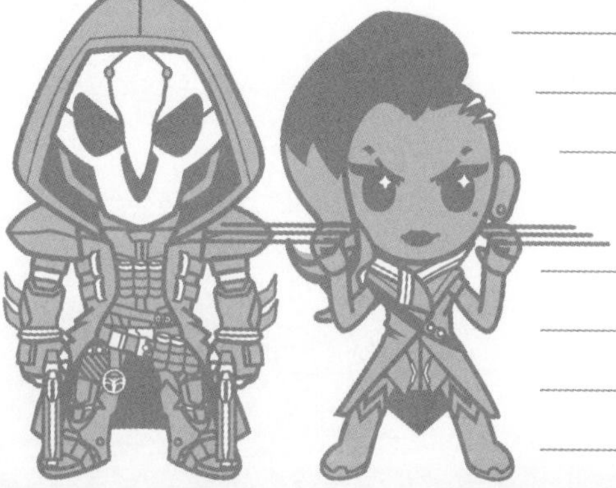

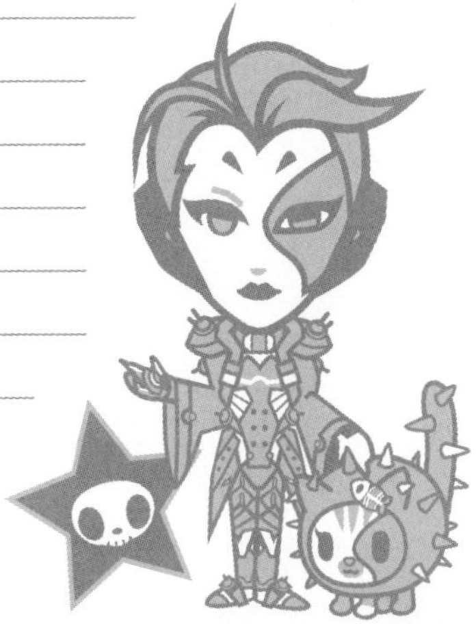

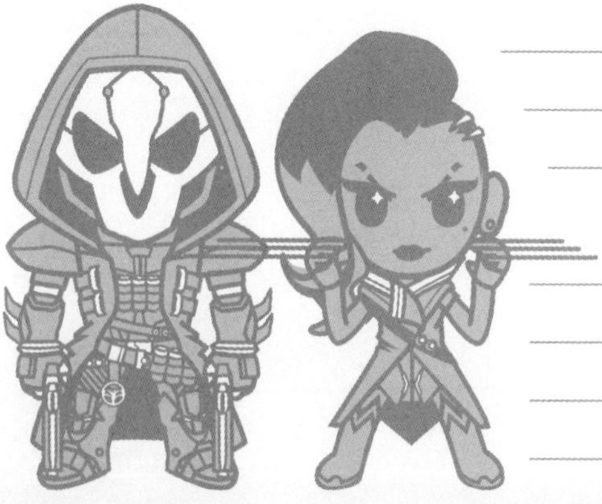

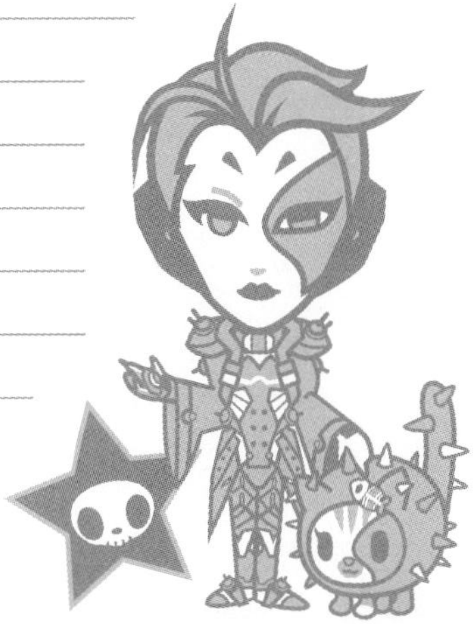

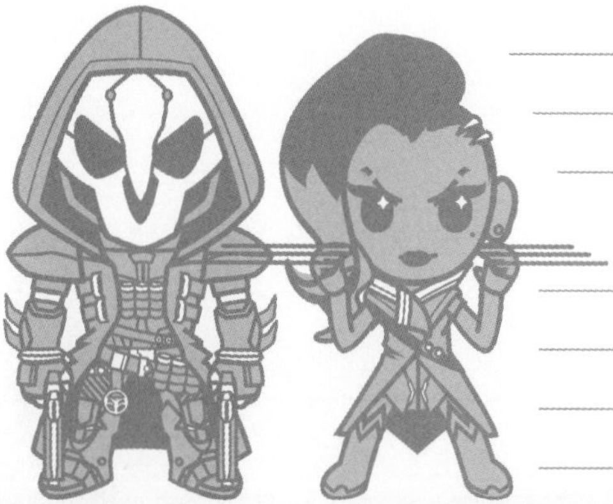

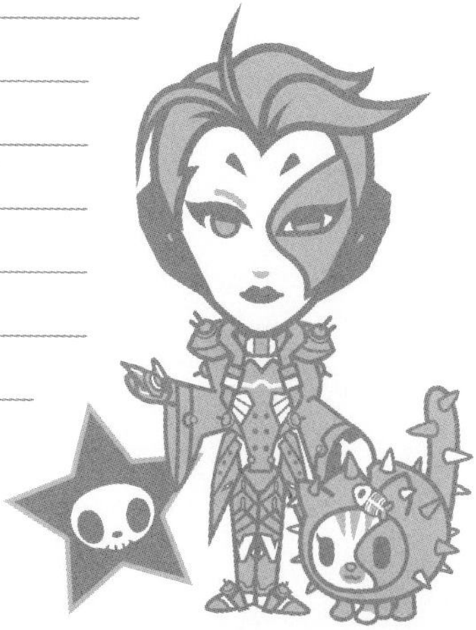

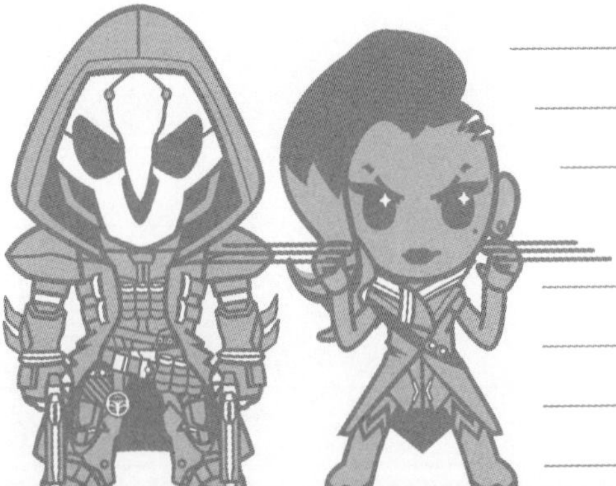

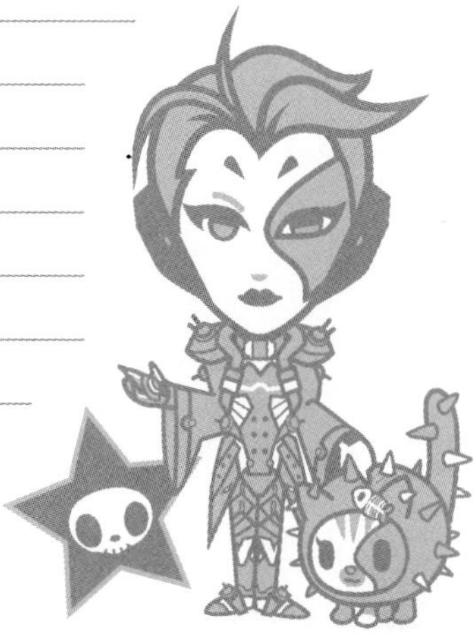

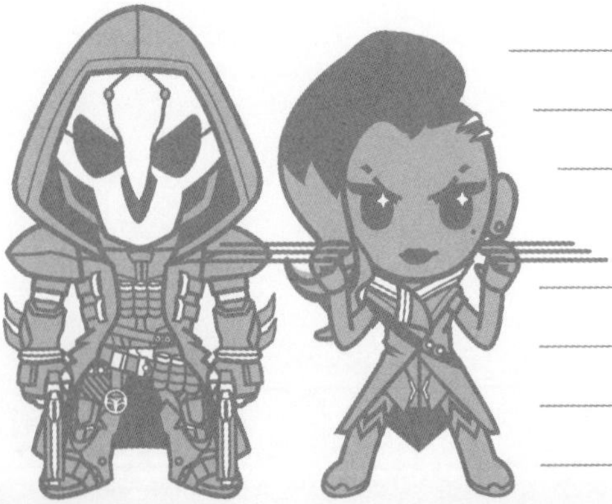

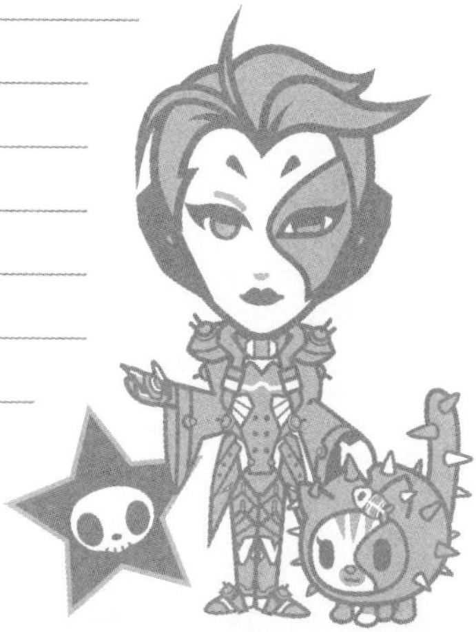

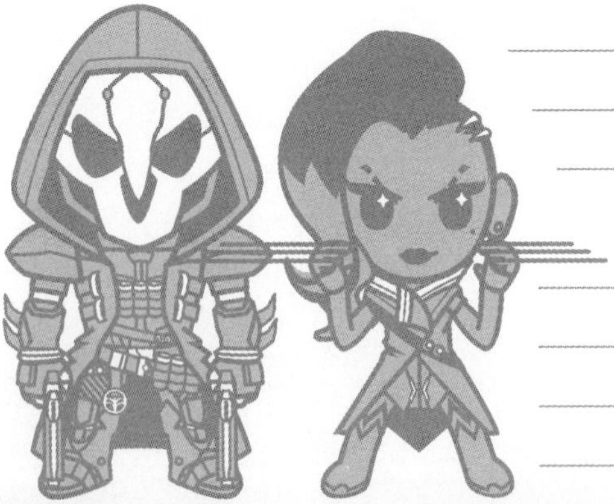

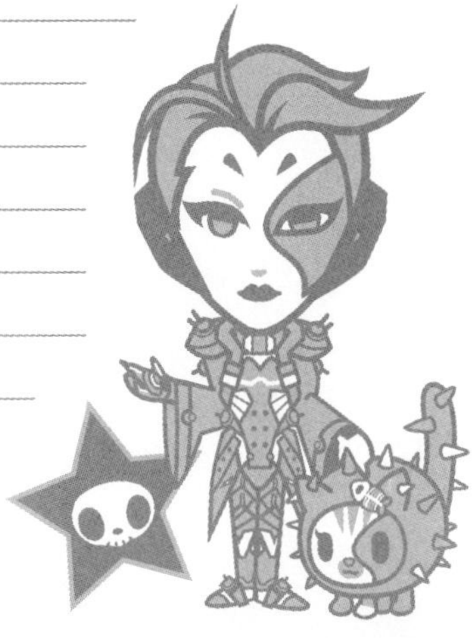

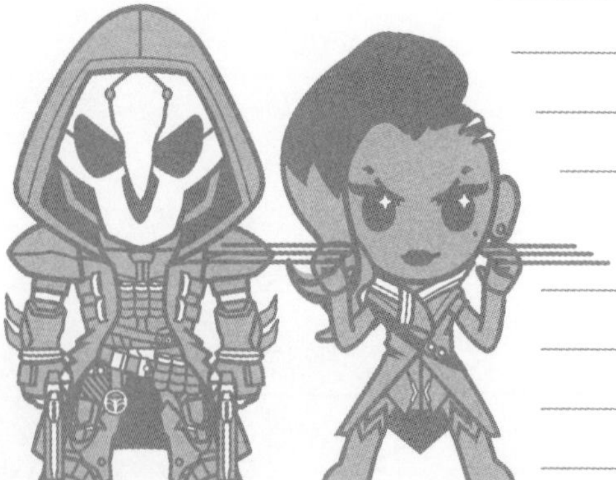

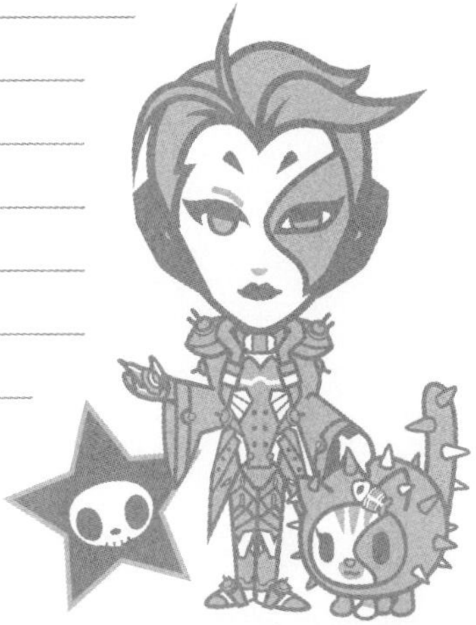

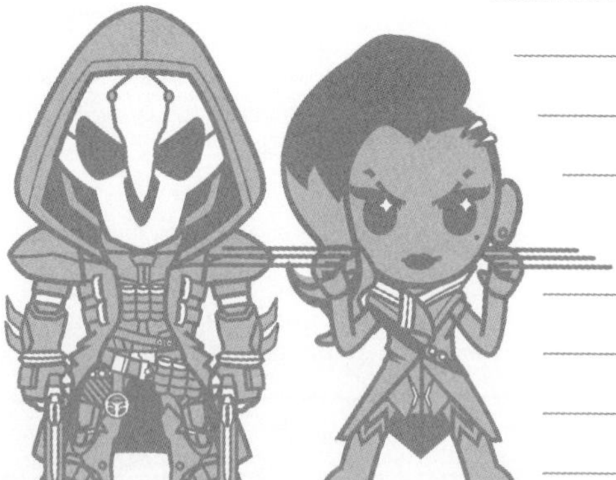

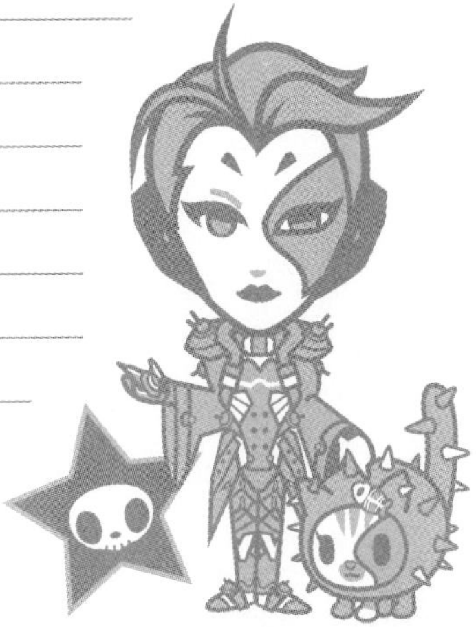

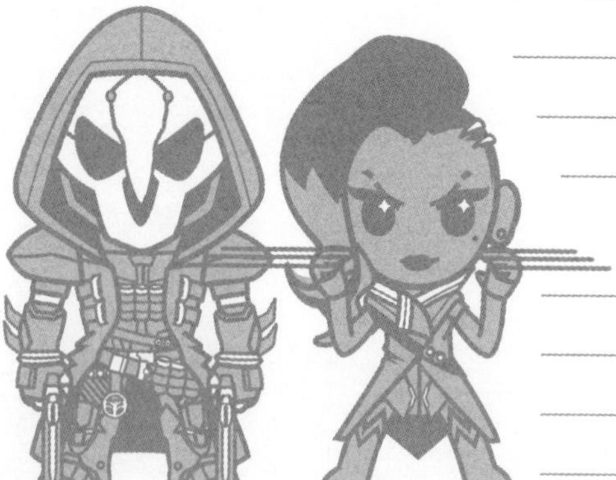

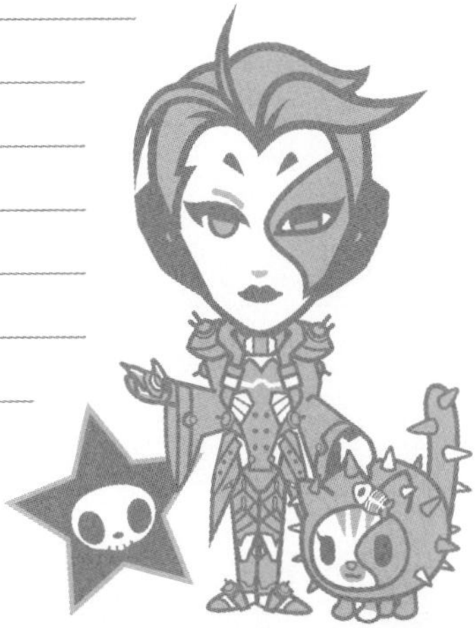

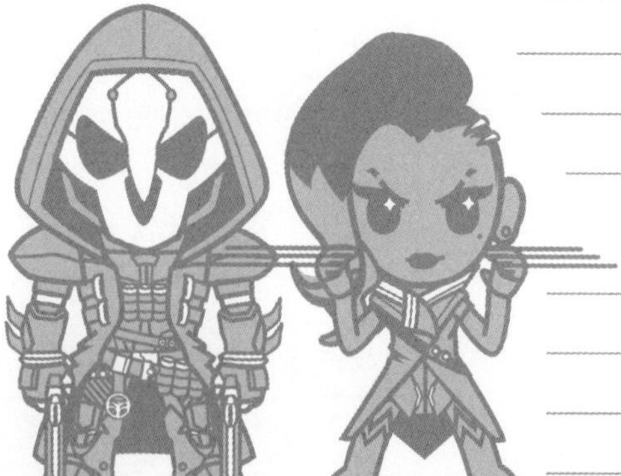

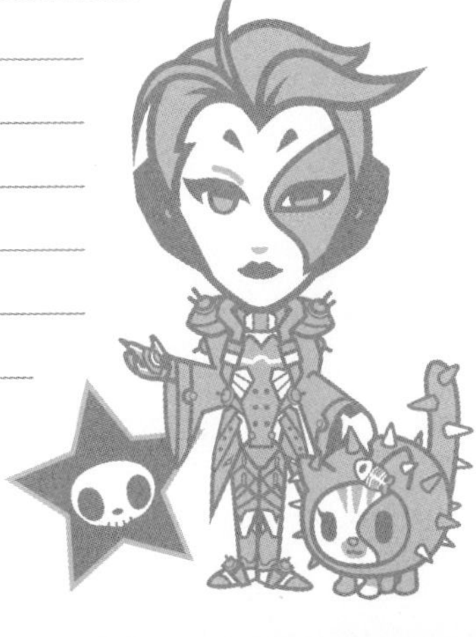

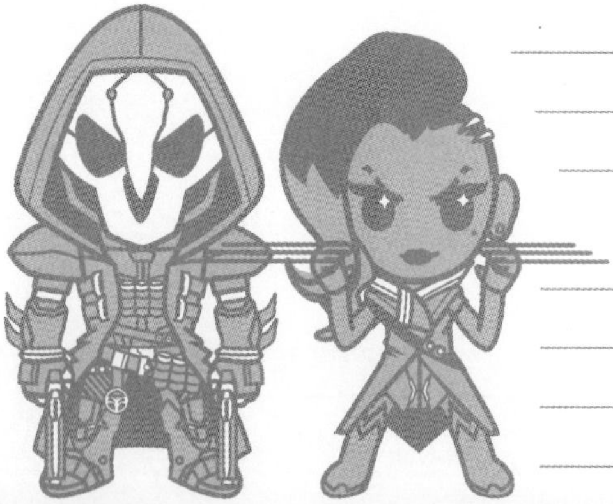

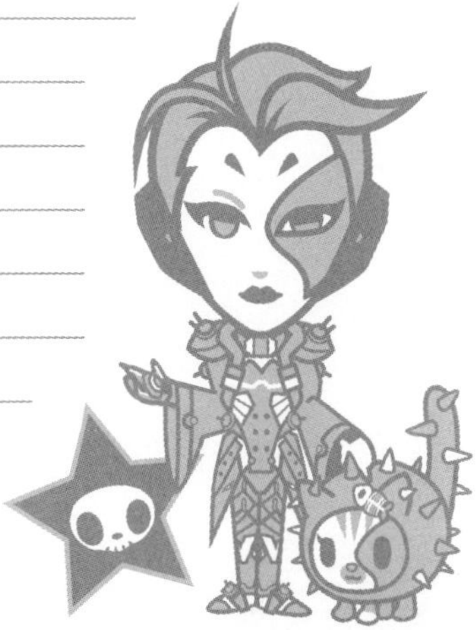

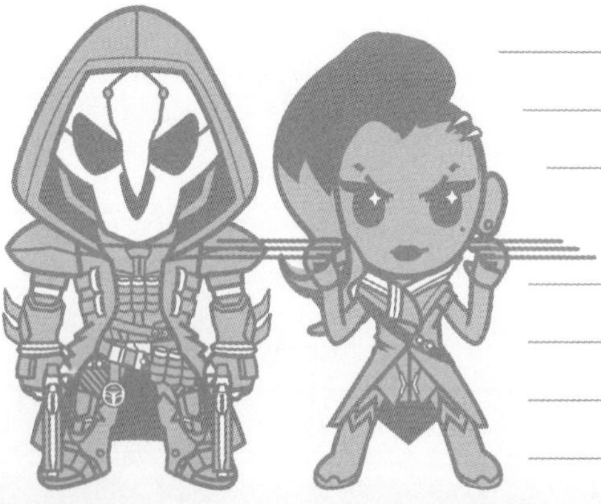

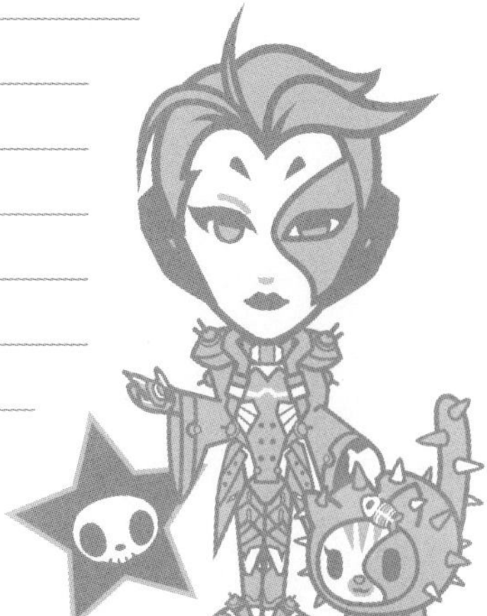

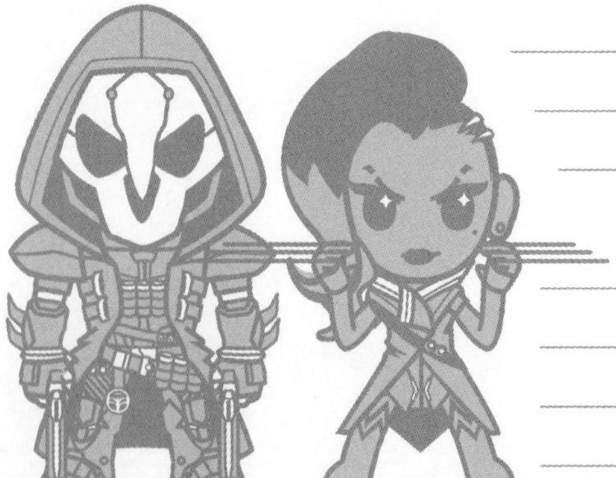

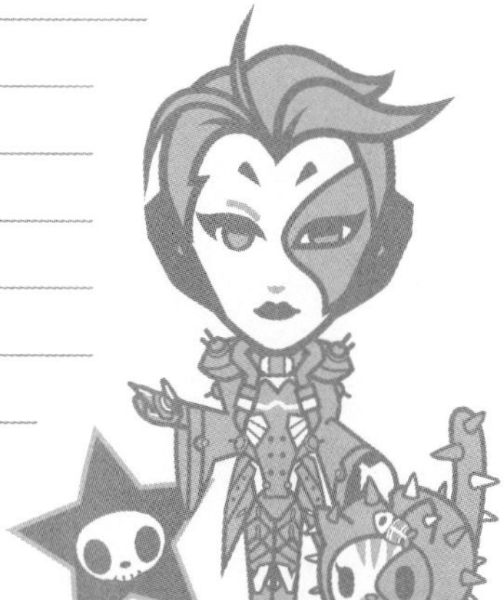

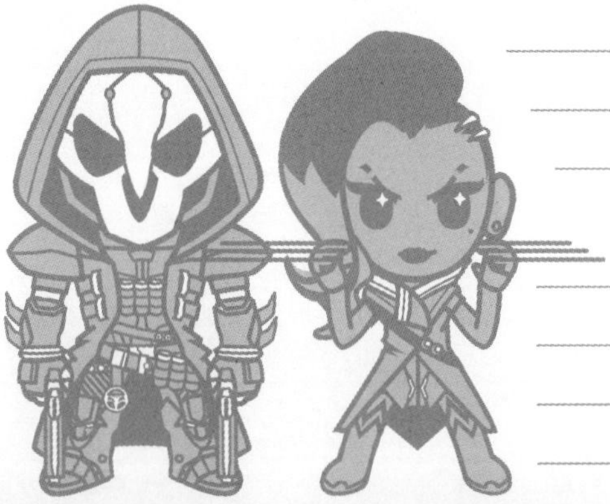

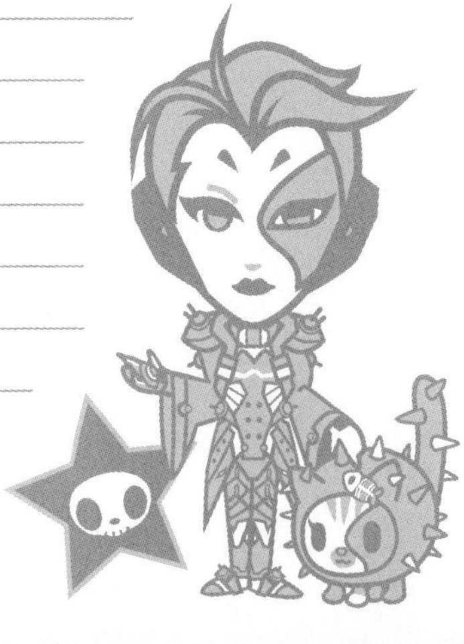

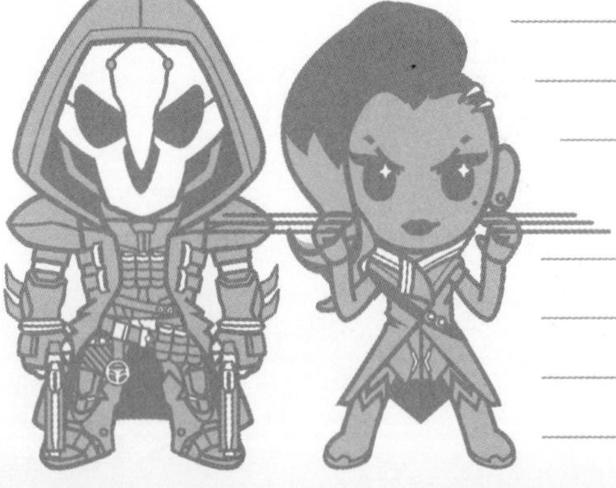

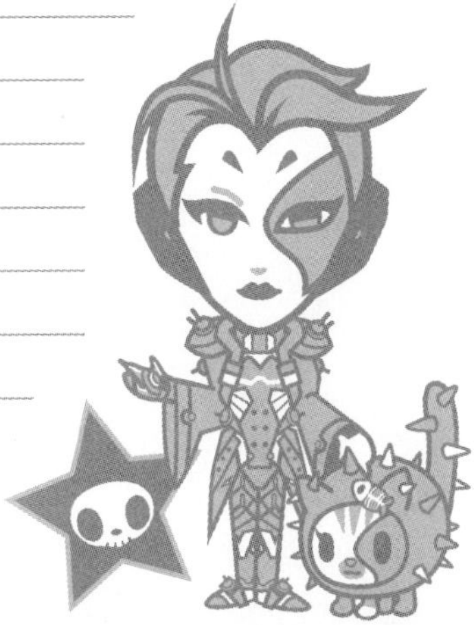

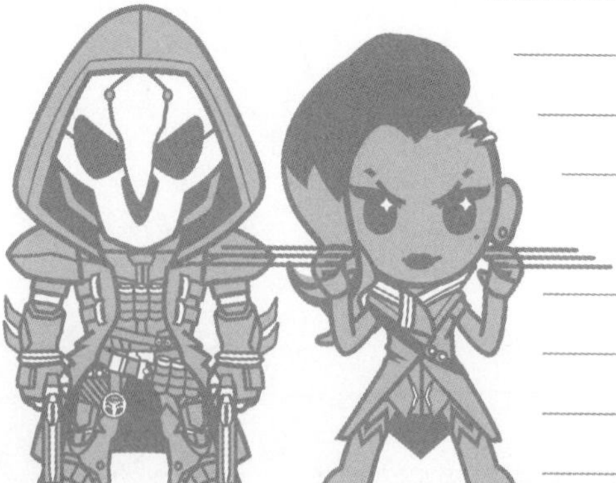

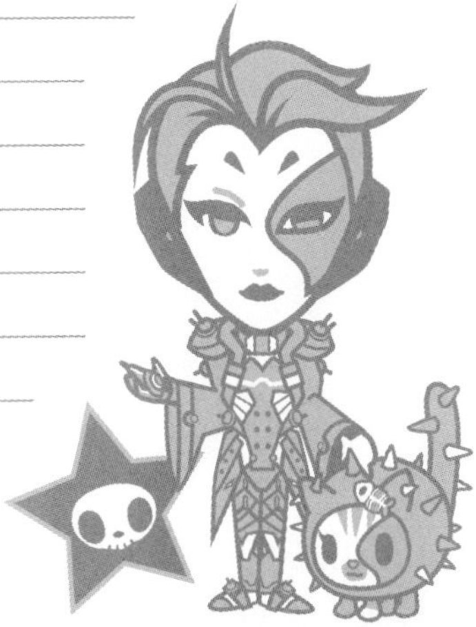

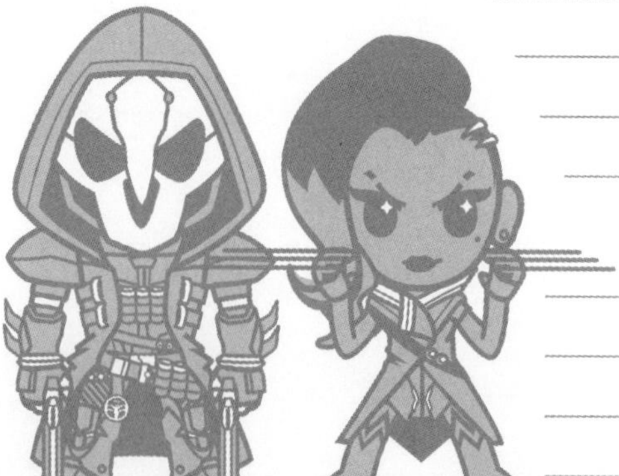

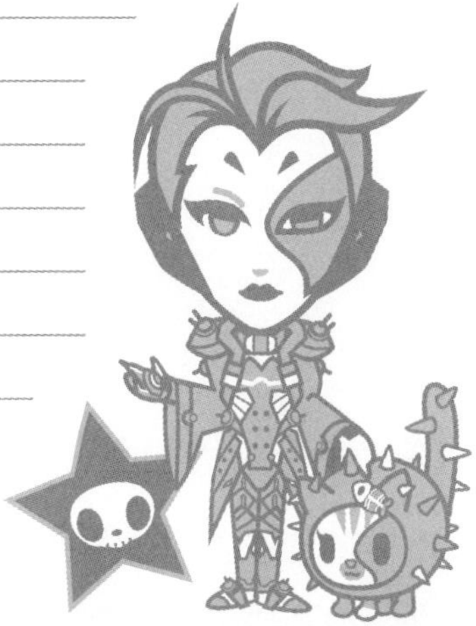

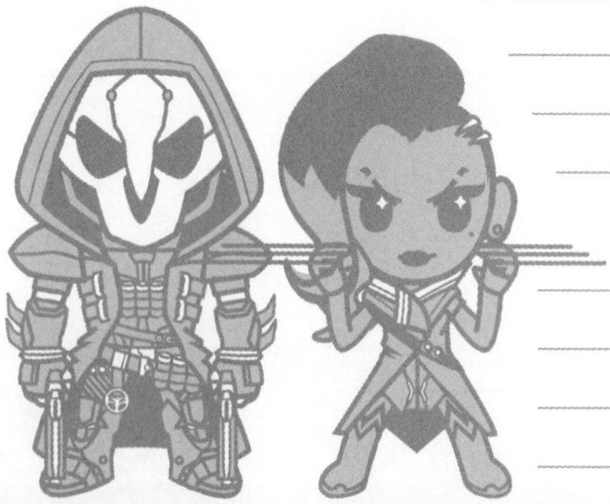

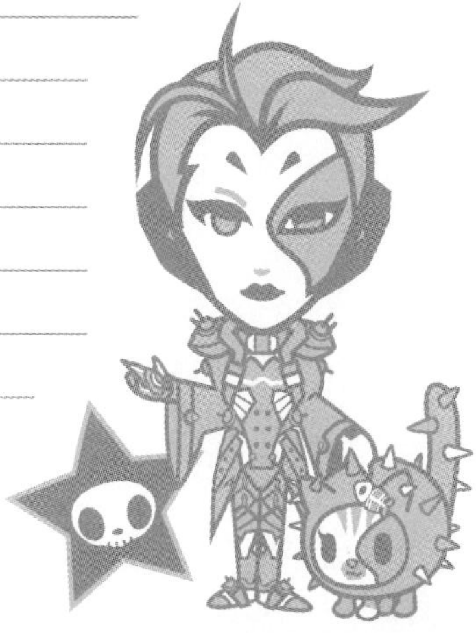

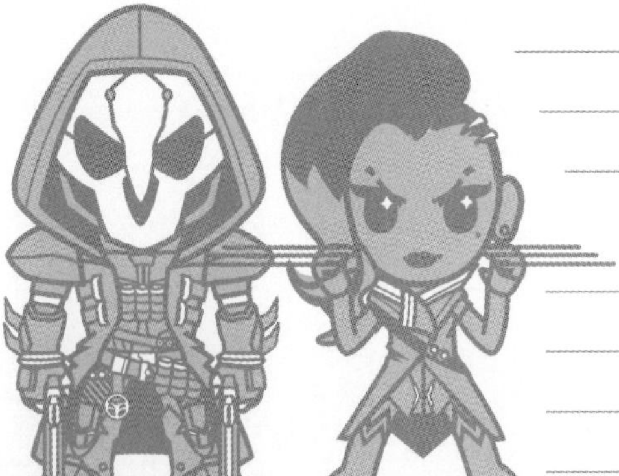

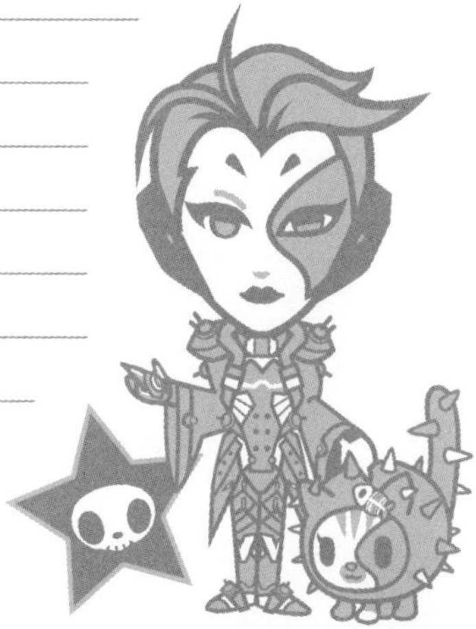

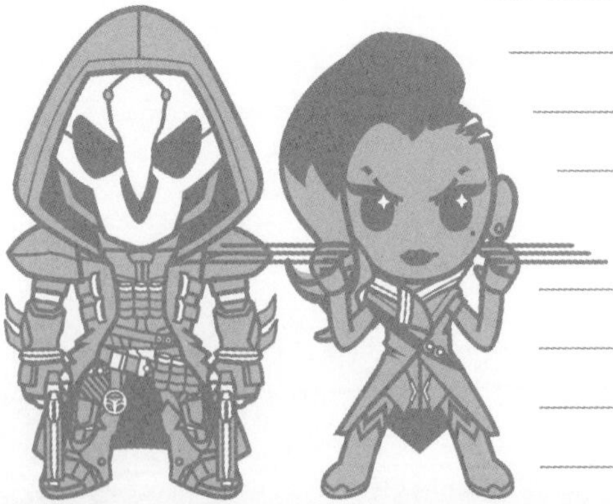

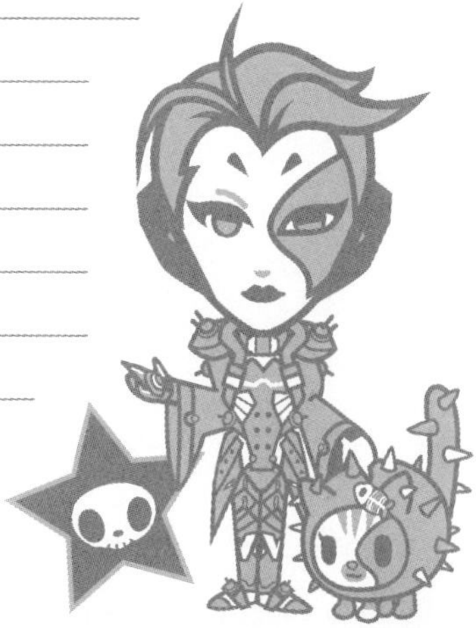

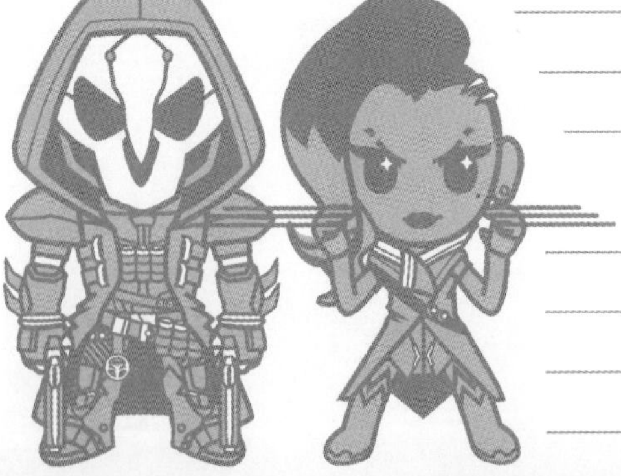

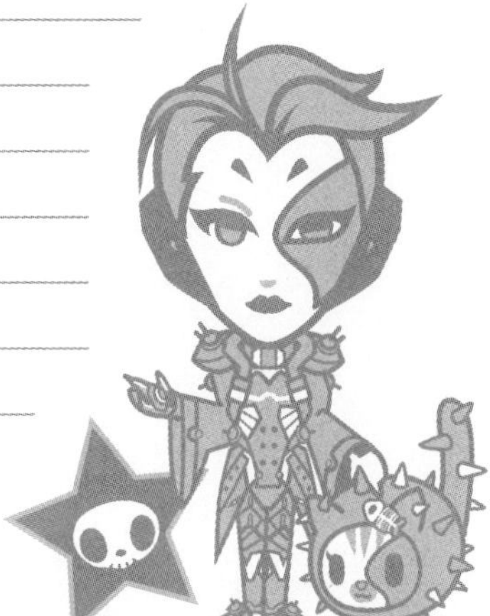

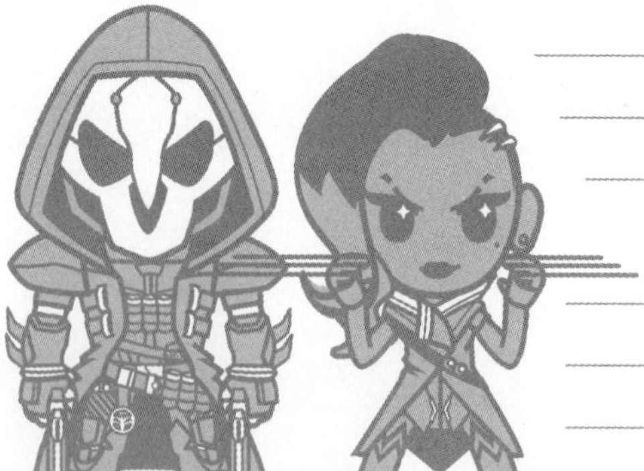

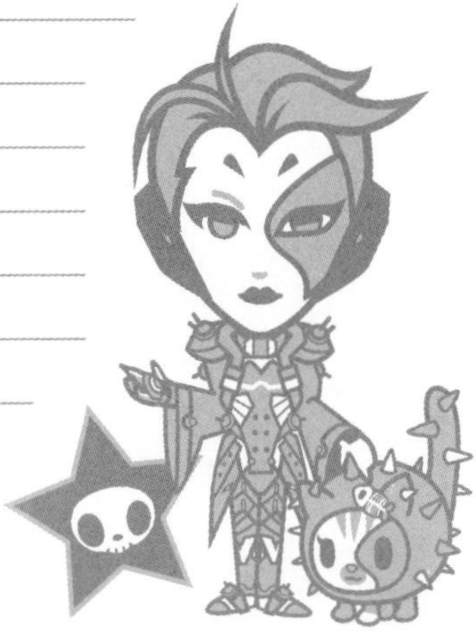

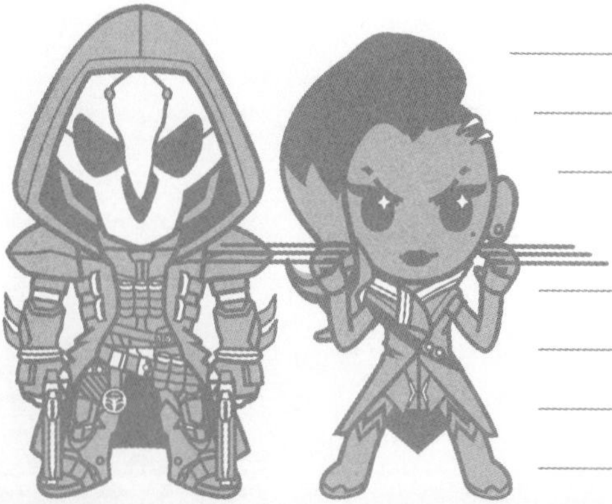

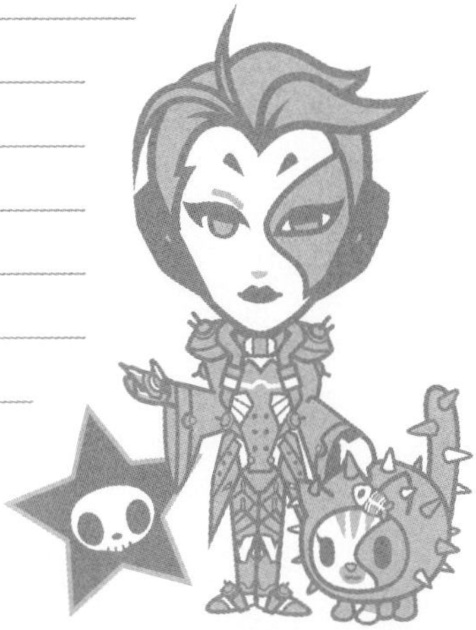

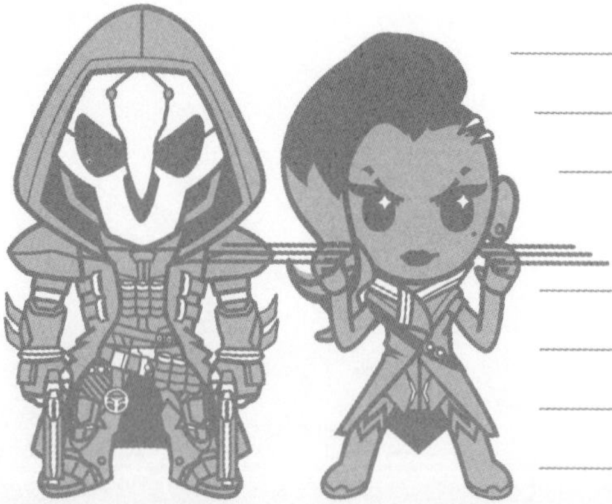

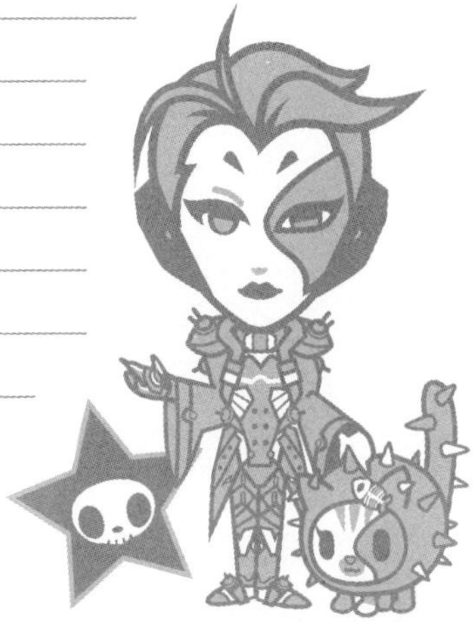

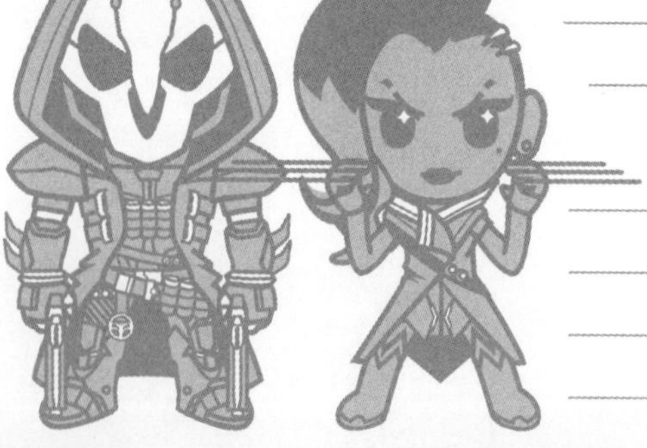

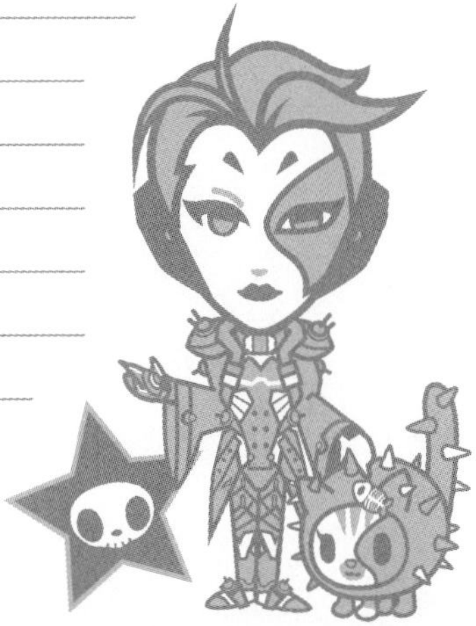

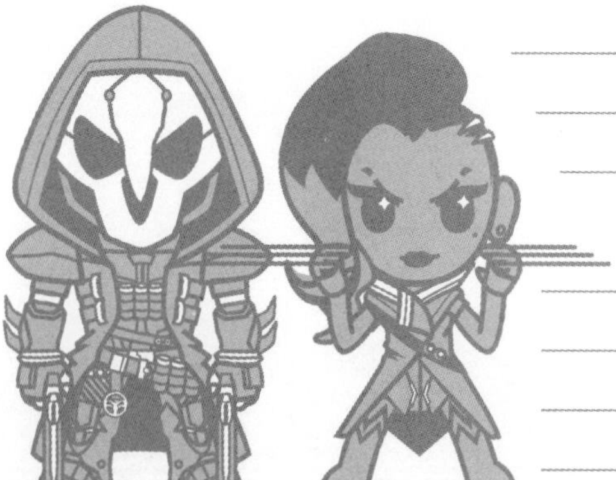

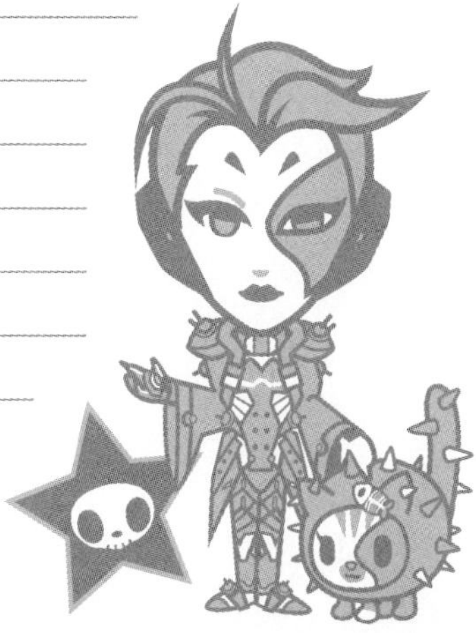

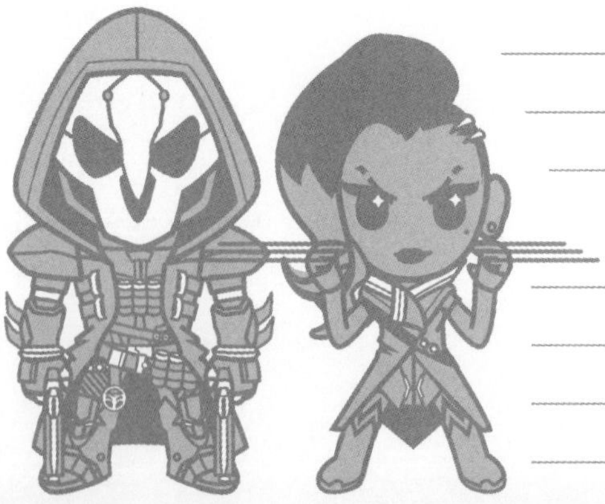

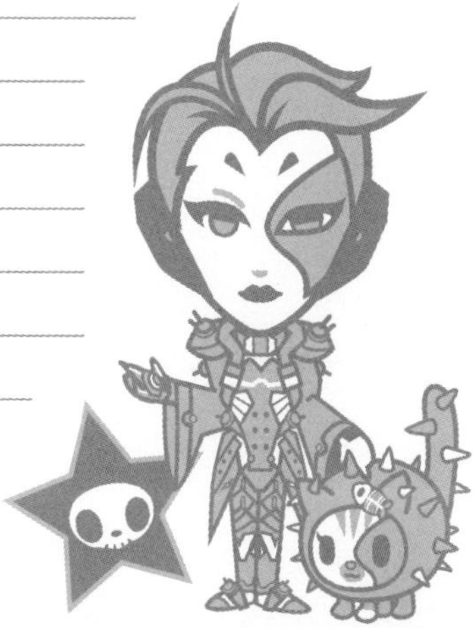

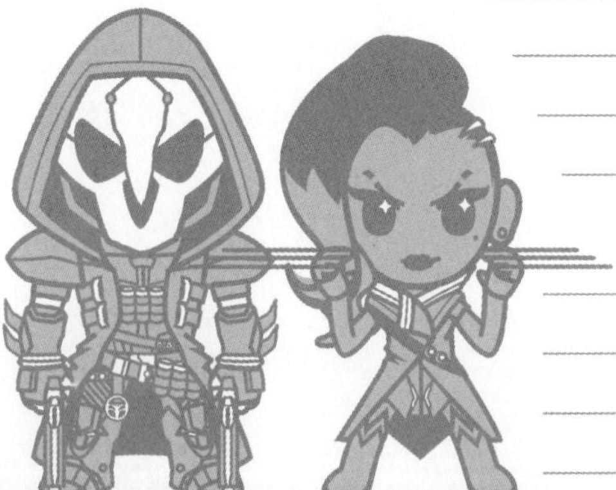

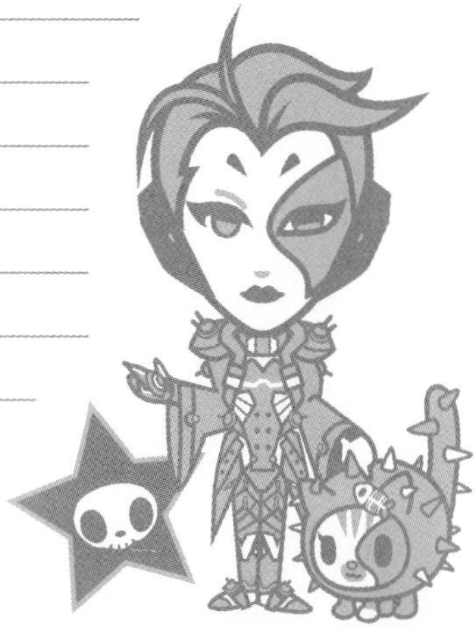

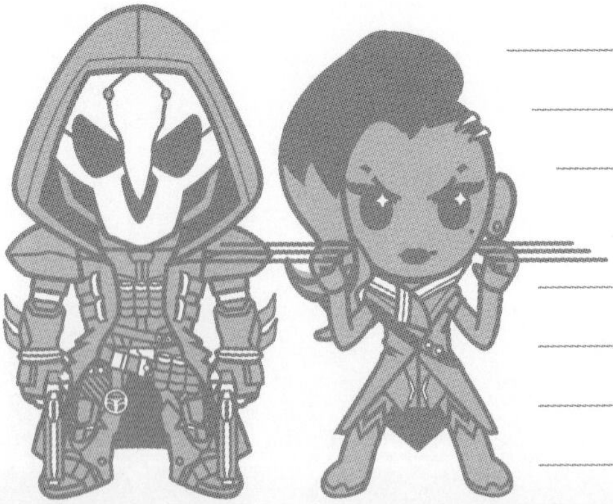

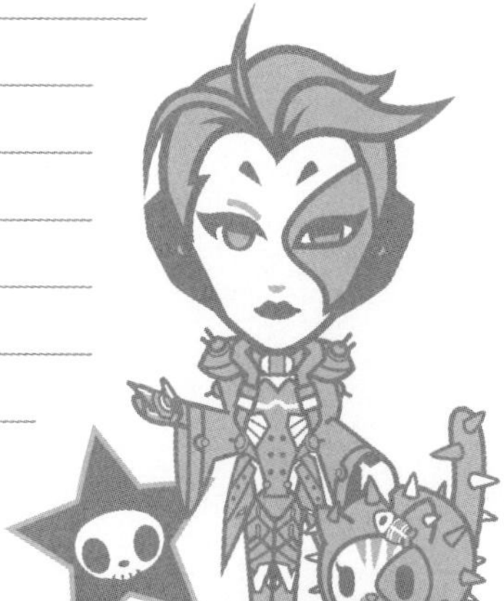

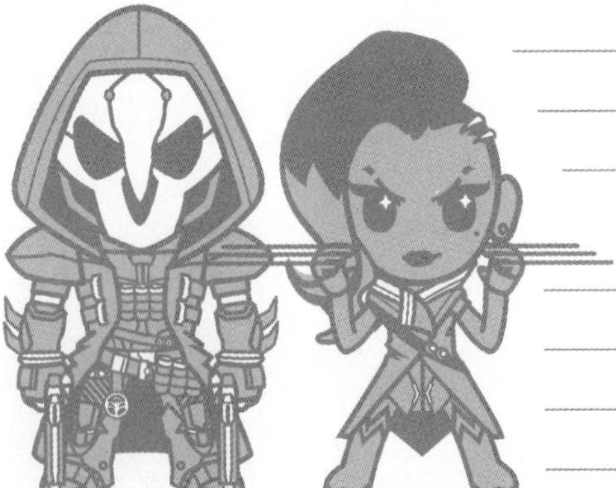

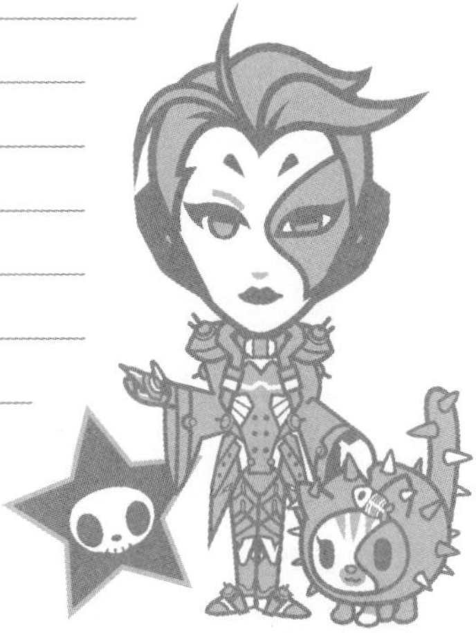

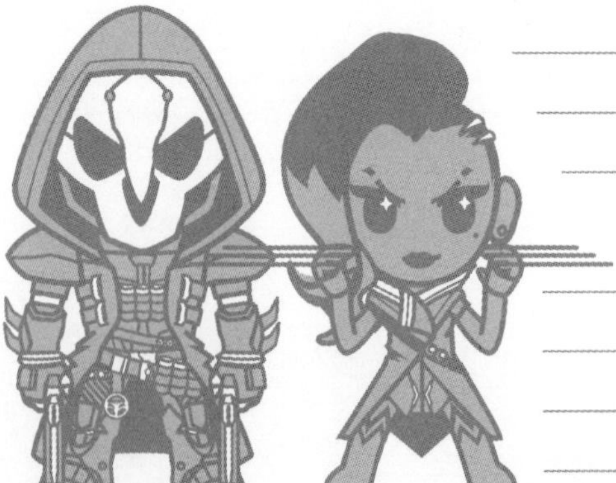

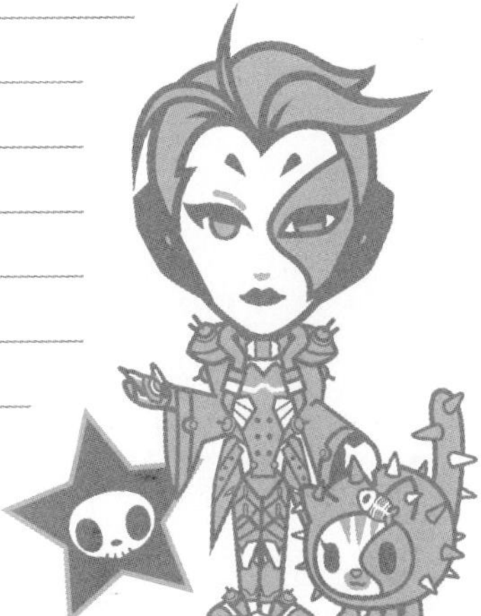

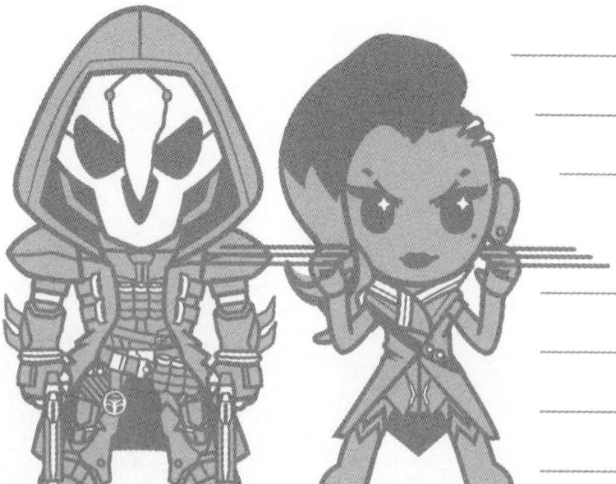

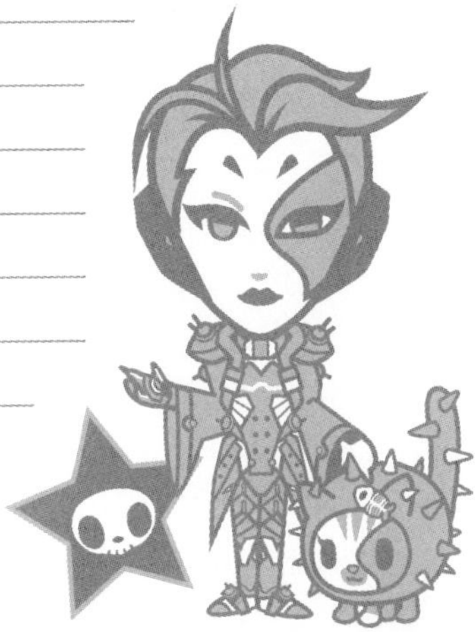

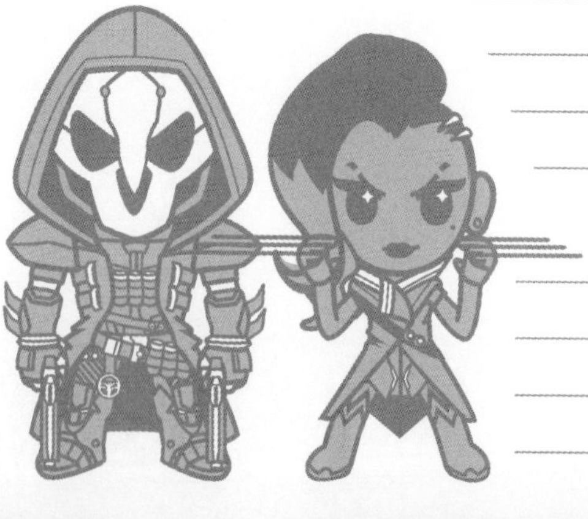

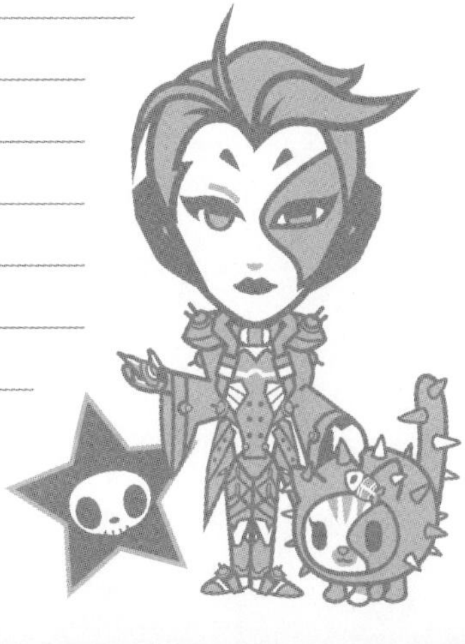

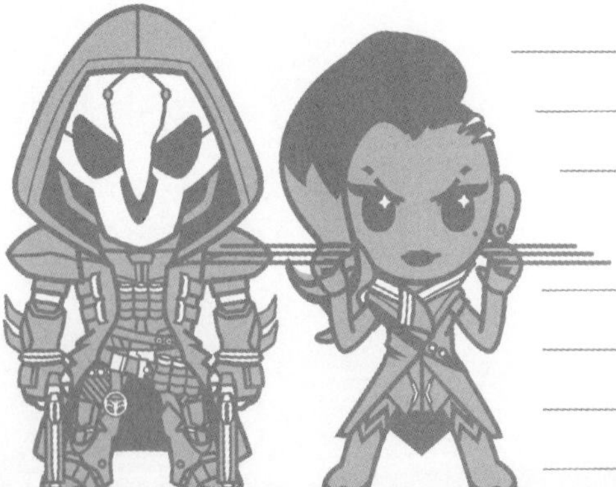

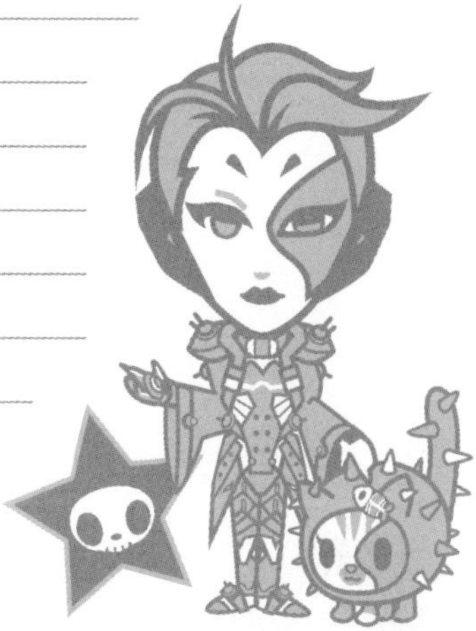

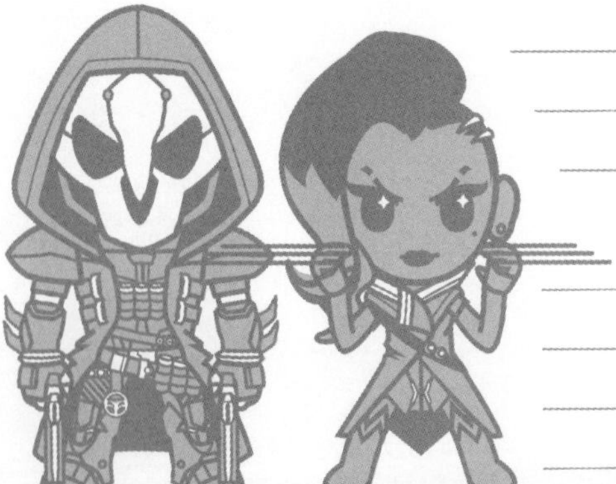

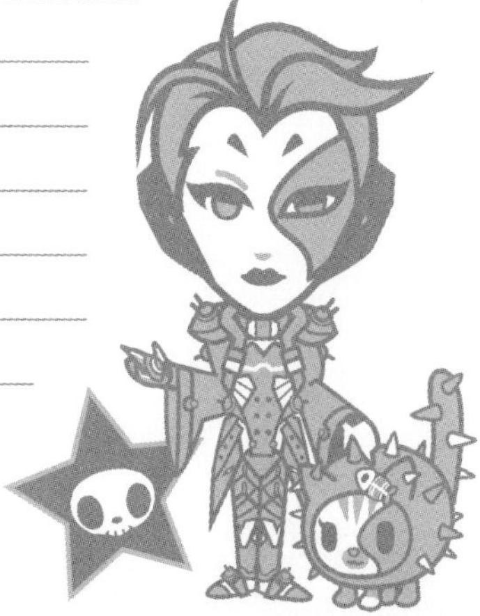

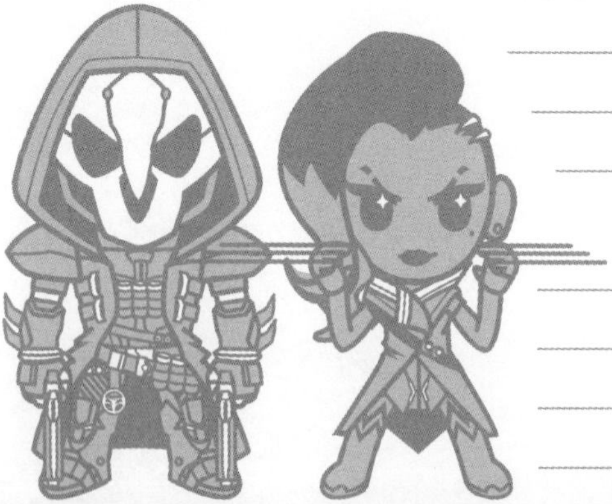

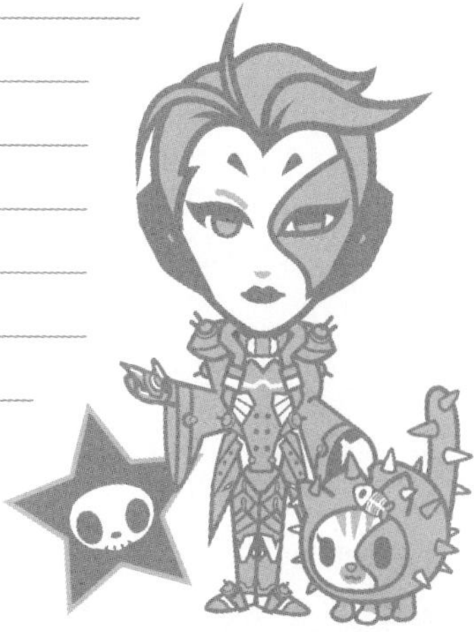

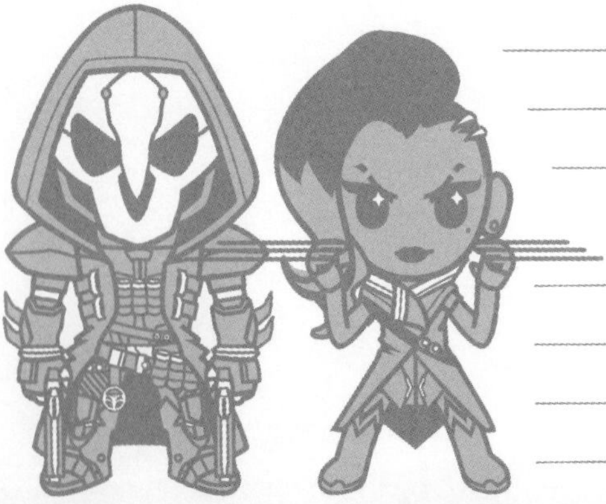

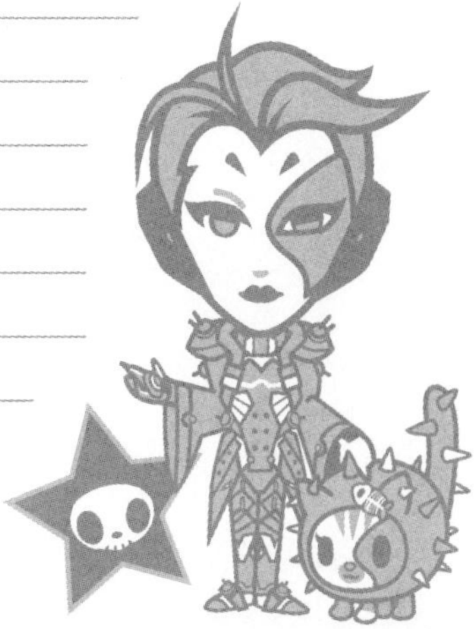

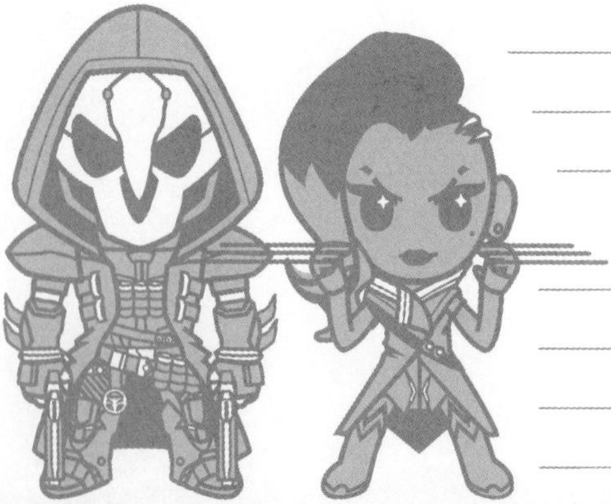

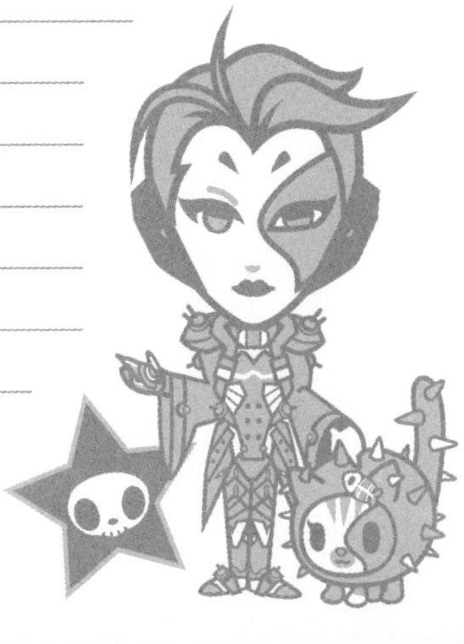

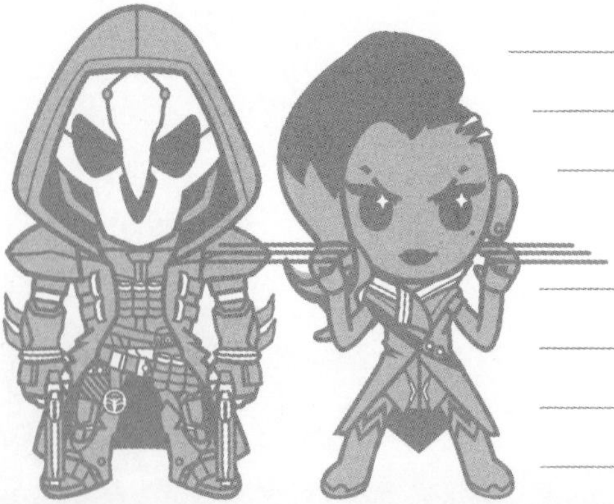

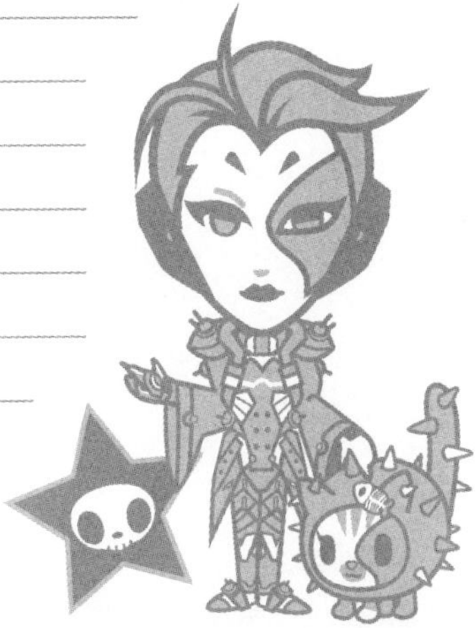

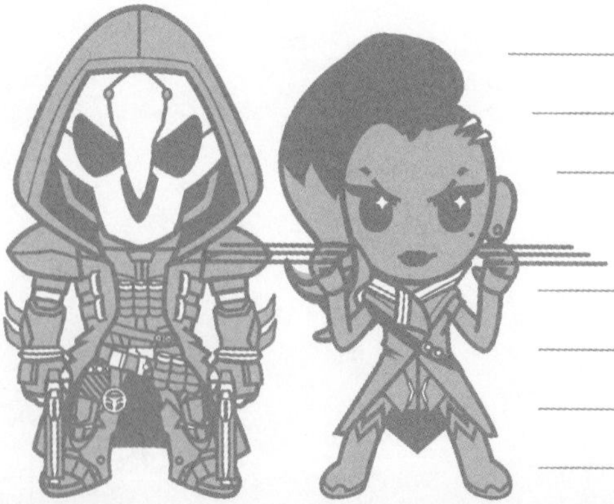

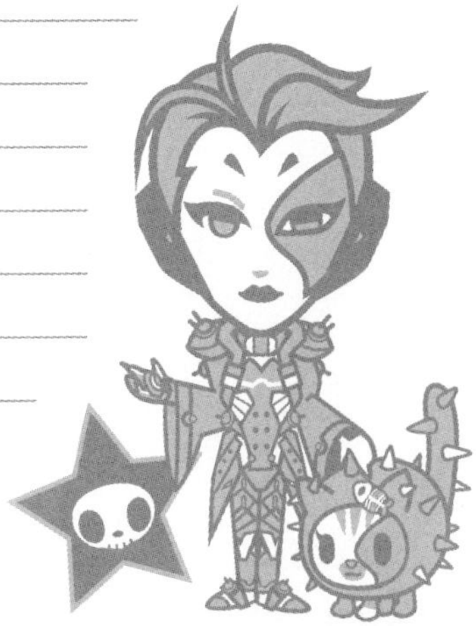

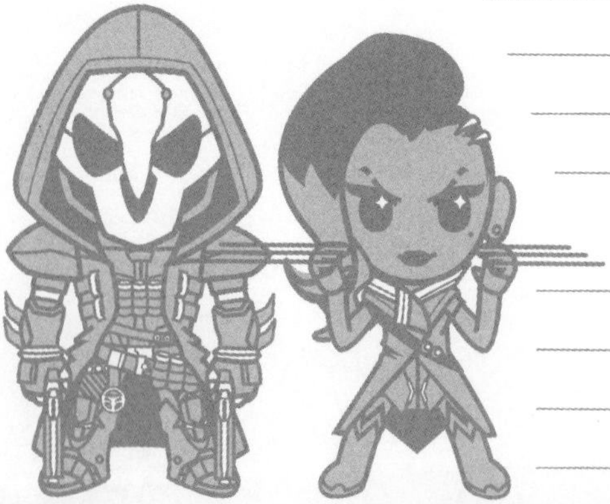

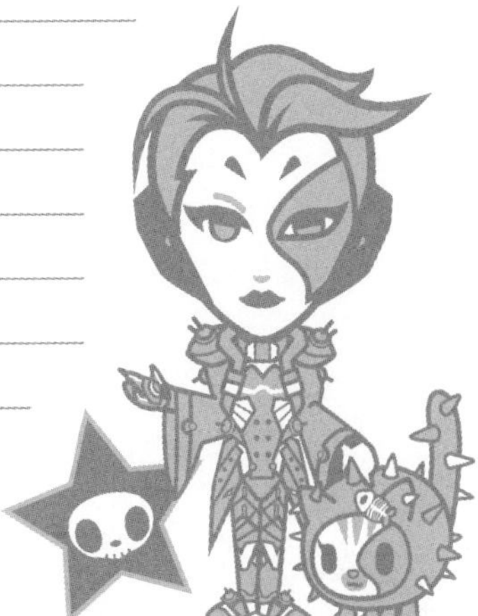

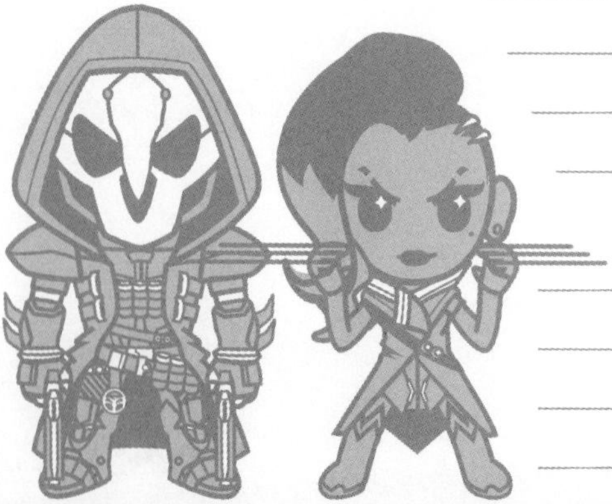

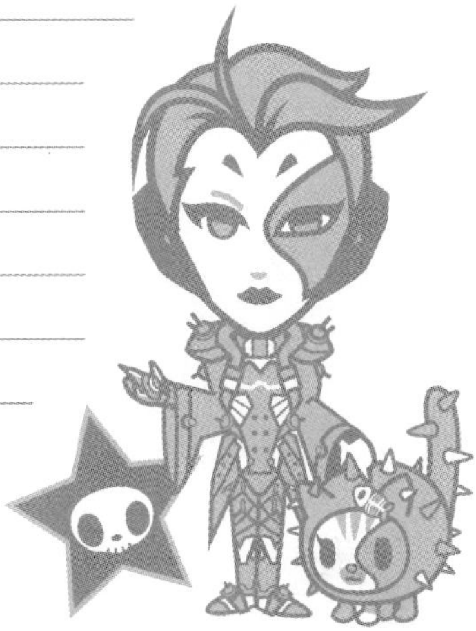

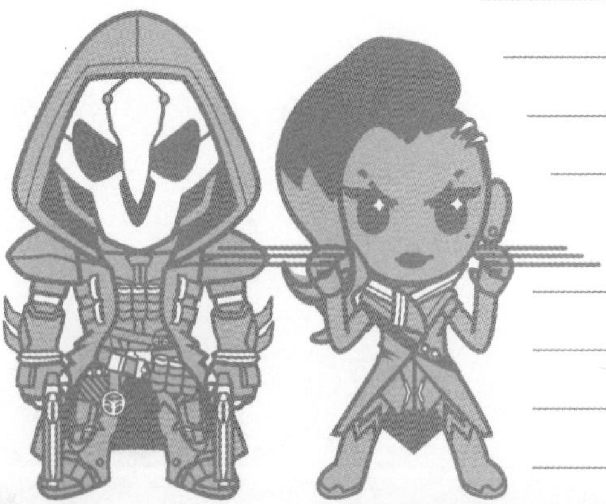

PROTEIN
MILK
BYE